Travel in the Mouth of the Wolf

Travel in the Mouth of the Wolf

Paul Fattaruso

Soft Skull Press • Brooklyn, NY • 2004

Travel in the Mouth of the Wolf
ISBN: 1-932360-49-2
©2004 by Paul Fattaruso
Cover Photograph ©2004 by John Fattaruso
Author Photograph ©2004 by Kristin Fattaruso

Book Design by David Janik
ShortLit Series Design by David Janik and Charles Orr

Published by Soft Skull Press • www.softskull.com
Distributed by Publishers Group West • www.pgw.com

Printed in Canada

Cataloging in Publication information for this book is
available from the Library of Congress

One. Iple's Memory

Iple walked and as he walked, having nothing specific to look at, only the vast abstract waves of ice and icy sky, he took unsystematic stock of his memories. He remembered standing at the window, the sun high, the sunlight with the worn-in gold of early afternoon, glowing, holy green lawns, cars driving past, though now he could pick out only one, a beige, preconscious BMW from the early 1980s, and evenly distributed, indeterminate pedestrians, and a vague, refreshed taste of water in his mouth and the back of his nose. Iple wasn't sure what window he'd been standing at, though he had a feeling the floor was carpeted in thick burgundy and the curtains royal blue with little white evenly distributed flowers, and he was unsure if he was remembering when he was six or when he was thirty, whether the car had maybe been from the late 1960s, whether it had driven past at all, or whether he was remembering an actual memory. What he remembered distinctly was the sense of fixity, brightness and inevitability, the slight sense of recognition that the moment would be remembered, unrecognizably.

Iple had thousands of memories like this one. They weren't enough to make a single childhood story out of. He remembered being curled on a cool linoleum floor with abdominal pains, wearing black pajamas with white pinstripes, and a sudden, unexpected sympathy from the linoleum, and nothing else. He used to check his wardrobe for a remembered pair of pajamas, empty his desk in search of a beautiful quill pen he remembered holding in his teeth late one night, hoping that the pen might give up some clue where it came from, why Iple had been holding it the way he had, hungry, from what he remembered, for a taco.

Two. Iple's Childhood

Iple walked and watched his breath curl out in long, momentary clouds, and tried to remember his childhood. He remembered his mother had worked wrapping chocolate bars to buy herself a beautiful purple bicycle when she was just a girl. He could still see her bicycle, which he knew he'd never seen, but could not remember the look of his mother, her alert eyes and her short tight curls of disorientingly black hair, her stewardess uniform in the far, dark corner of the closet, hanging over a pile of disused shoes, insinuating an invisible, unimaginable world folded into the actual one, or the gesture she used to flip a pancake.

He would test each memory by trying to imagine one of its opposites, his mother with her wild blonde pigtails, her calm, sleepy eyes, her closet of nothing but delicate nightgowns, too thin almost to touch, she who never wrapped a candy nor cared to own a bicycle, and each memory seemed as believable as the one before it. It was his sister who bought the bicycle, and the bicycle had been orange, if he'd had a sister.

Iple couldn't isolate a single certain detail of his personal history around which he might build some probable corollary memories, which he suspected might lead him to something else he could be sure of, a second certain detail, then a third, and so on; and after an initial panic, he wasn't especially inclined to keep trying. The cold froze the inside of his nose hard like a flowerpot.

Iple decided to be glad not to know where or how he grew up. For almost a minute, he hoped he'd had a happy childhood, and then he hoped for fifteen seconds that he hadn't, and then he lost interest in the question entirely.

Three. The Antarctica Decision

Iple can remember why he came to Antarctica. He was walking around his block to get an idea. The clouds hung fixed, dumpling-shaped, shadowlessly bright. An orange cat looked at Iple with the poker face of a cat refusing to give up its idea. The birds laughed at Iple. Iple carried a wooden ball-and-cup game that he liked to play to make himself look casual, like he wasn't looking for anything, and he used it now. A string joined the red wooden ball to the yellow wooden cup on its blue wooden handle. Iple held it by its blue handle and swung the red ball in an arc upward and tried to catch it on the way down in the yellow cup. The cup was just slightly too small for the ball to fit into.

I will tell you something that no one knows for sure. Time is discrete, like the frames in movies, still moments in progression. For Iple to swing the red ball to when it bounced off the rim of the yellow cup took only about five thousand moments, still too many to notice individually, no matter how closely you watch. From when the red ball bounced off the yellow cup to when the truck touched the pump in front of the gas station Iple was walking past was just under a thousand moments. It's hard to talk about just when the truck touched the pump, since unlike time, space is continuous, and the closer you look, the more difficult it is to tell exactly when a thing is touching another thing and when a thing is not.

It took about four hundred moments from when the truck first touched the pump to the height of the explosion. The explosion killed five people and badly burned two. It killed the orange cat. It takes five whole moments for a thing to go from living to dead. It took twenty-six moments for Iple's hearing to go from normal human hearing to no hearing.

Iple should have been dead or badly burned. The bones in his ear felt hot, like they would burn through his head, but he could still think. He looked unscathed and sat down on the curb across the street. He sat there a long time, and the clouds kept looking like dumplings and didn't go anywhere or reshape themselves. Firefighters and paramedics came and did everything they could. Policemen came and asked questions. Iple pointed to his right ear and shook his head.

Iple watched the gas station and environs until everything was gone from it, and then watched until a bird landed for a minute and left again, which reminded him of how to leave, and he got up and went to a little traincar diner.

Iple pointed to the Monte Cristo on the menu. He didn't want to try speaking. His ears felt less hot, and he could think more. He thought to walk around until morning. In the morning, he thought to turn everything he had into money. Then he thought to rent a little room in an old janitor's attic and learn all he could about Antarctica and keep eating sandwiches.

Upon becoming an Antarctica expert, Iple still did not understand why people went there. He joined a group of scientists and went there.

Four. Zebedee

Zebedee was a gifted gambler. His first time in a casino he won until the casino men asked him to leave and not come back. They watched Zebedee for a long time for cheating, then they took him to a room and had him empty his pockets on the table. They had him take off his jacket. Zebedee wore a camel-colored jacket. Then they told him to take off his sky-colored shirt, and Zebedee said, "Please, gentlemen, this is absurd."

The casino men told Zebedee what they thought was absurd, and that was how much Zebedee won in the casino. They were going to find out how he cheated. Zebedee looked like he was cheating when he gambled, because he didn't pay close attention. He studied the light fixtures, a lady's necklace, the drinks going by on trays, their ice and their straws, their cherries and pineapple slices and olives and pearl onions.

Zebedee said, "I am too embarrassed for you to keep your money. You may have it back, and I will be going," and he put his arms both at once back into his jacket sleeves. One casino man said it was too late for that, but halfheartedly, and Zebedee walked out the door. Before he disappeared completely through the door, the casino man said don't ever come back to this casino.

Zebedee went home and grew a mustache, a swooping handlebar. He went back to the casino and won once on a slot machine and left, the pockets of his camel jacket swollen and jangling.

Five. More About Zebedee

Zebedee learned how to gamble inconspicuously, a little at a time, first a little blackjack, then a little roulette. He drew attention to himself only one other time. When he was twenty, he took Charlotte, the judge's daughter, to the diner and to a drive-in movie. Afterwards he took her with him to the roulette table and bet zero twenty times in a row, little bets, and she watched it come up zero twenty times in a row, and everyone else at the table afraid to really bet zero because there is no way it can come up zero again, not after six in a row. Not after fourteen in a row. Charlotte must have squeezed Zebedee's arm and bent her knees into a near-curtsey with excitement about fifty times, and each time it made it harder for Zebedee not to keep betting zero. But they were little bets, so when it was over everyone at the table walked away feeling it was just a small if essential chink taken out of their ethos.

Charlotte had little tiny ears and great big lips and an astonishingly swoopy waist and hips and a paunch and she picked out maidenly dresses to wear for Zebedee, and when Zebedee saw her in one of her dresses he would twist one end of his mustache and love Charlotte, and she loved him, for the way things seemed to want to happen well for him.

Then in February Charlotte got on a plane to Oahu with her father the judge, and the pilot flew it on purpose into the water, straight and fast. Zebedee thought, what if he had bet on her return, and why hadn't he.

Zebedee felt sick gambling, and took back his job tossing dough at the pizzeria. Then four years later he felt better enough to gamble again. He went to horse races and dog races and once to a chicken fight in Louisiana. He watched the women in large hats, the men in bow ties, a lonely girl working the betting booth, a pickpocket, sometimes the horses or dogs or chickens. He bet long shots, trifectas of long shots.

He never bet on real events, the birth of a nephew, or that Charlotte would walk out of the Pacific Ocean and into the Baja, not even out of breath.

He traveled and did favors, and everyone loved him. He traveled so he could buy gifts—novel, beautiful things for his brothers and sisters and nieces and nephews and Esther who owned the pizzeria and her boy Gottlieb. He brought back fireworks, swords, coins, a rickshaw, an Aztec spoon, a Fabergé egg for Esther, a Go set for Gottlieb, with an ebony board and pieces made of brilliant, polished coral.

Zebedee's hair went white, but his mustache stayed black. Gottlieb met a girl to marry, with irises the color of sand, which Zebedee found sweetly treacherous, and on the day before the wedding, Gottlieb said to Zebedee, I am very busy and can you do me the favor of driving these chickens to my mother? And Zebedee said, "Of course, Gottlieb," and driving the truck full of chickens his eyes clouded over and his balance clouded over, and he sent the truck straight into a gas pump, destroying himself and the chickens and the orange cat and ruining Iple's ears.

Six. How Great Things Are Done

With nothing but a swift horse. With nothing but a paper clip and a stick of chewing gum. With nothing but a compass. With nothing but a bright light and a penny whistle. With nothing but a pocket watch, a glass of water, and a match. With nothing but a kite and a loose tooth. With nothing but a breeze and a handkerchief. With nothing but a bowl of oatmeal. With nothing but a wedding ring and a postcard. With nothing but a pair of owls. With nothing but an apple, a river, and a handful of pine needles. With nothing but a bullet and a sewing kit. With nothing but a football helmet, a roman candle, and a padlock. With nothing but half a map. With nothing but a boot and a sword. With nothing but a stray dog and a strip of bacon. With nothing but hair off the barber's floor. With nothing but an idle lie and a milkshake. With nothing but a bite of rumaki. With nothing but a dowel and a bandsaw. With nothing but a chocolate grasshopper. With nothing but a square meter of plate glass. With nothing but a cell. With nothing but a cart. With nothing but a potato. With nothing but a potato bug.

Seven. The Ice Station

A big helicopter with two propellers dropped the team of scientists onto Antarctica, and Iple with them. Another big helicopter dropped a whole bunch of boxes full of the things the scientists figured they needed to survive (beans, Sterno). The fanciest thing was an auger that Wes, the humanist psychologist, brought to dig deep reservoirs for the outhouses. It took Wes a week to put the auger together, while everyone else was working on the igloos, and once it got running, he used it to take off his right arm at the elbow.

Wes didn't make a sound. He lay down in the snow and bled and cried a little to himself, and by the time Justin the photojournalist found him they all thought it was too late, but somehow Tina the doctor saved Wes. They had a toast to Tina in the central igloo and drank red wine and ate Brie with roasted red peppers and baguette.

Each night, Penelope the microbiologist played soft songs on her flügelhorn in the central igloo, where she took her turn watching over Wes, under a pile of blankets, his face gone light gray and fevered, sweating, by the fire. And each night, from his igloo, Iple thought he could just almost make out Penelope's song, round and muted, through the nothing he could hear.

In the morning, Iple walked far off from camp, with a sandwich folded into his parka and a Thermos of tea, until the village of igloos was gone over the horizon, and then on to where there was only the snow, and the sky reflecting snow, until it seemed fair not to hear anything. Then he sat down, took his tea and sandwich, and rocked himself a little in the cradle of blank, easeful lifelessness. This was the only time Iple's mind did not revolt against his body.

The days got longer, and for a while Iple stayed out as long as it was day. The team of scientists worried about him, especially Asa the architect, who had come to realize his village of igloos. They worried that Iple might not come back, but mostly they worried over any strange behavior, any trace of madness. There were six psychologists other than Wes, all of them watching for new symptoms, and only the old man, Benjamin the behaviorist psychologist, insisted on Iple's sanity. "He's an odd bastard, but harmless," Benjamin said at lunch, "unlike this puerile nimrod," pointing his croissant at Asa, "who is determined to ruin my back in these demented, midget igloos." Benjamin was eighty-nine and six-foot-nine. At Tina's toast, he declared, "I am amazed that the lady doctor has managed to save this stunning nincompoop."

Eight. Benjamin and Penelope

Benjamin was ever noticeably kind only to Penelope the micro-biologist. On Sunday mornings he made her eggs Benedict. Penelope's igloo was near the kitchen igloo, and she woke instinctively at the faint smell of hollandaise sauce and came to the kitchen igloo and ate, still cloudy-eyed from sleep, and Benjamin would ask her what she'd been dreaming about, with yes and no questions, and Penelope nodded or shook her head, wrapped in a tangle of hair.

Benjamin had almost three hundred grandchildren. Penelope was the first one he knew about, and the sixth over-all. Wes the humanist psychologist was third overall. The girl who married Gottlieb was one-hundred-fifty-first overall and second in a set of triplets.

As the days got longer and the nights almost unnoticeable, Benjamin was the most careful to keep a schedule and to sleep like the nights kept coming. He had a rowing machine and a juicemaker and four cats and nine gerbils to keep track of. He hoped to find out if Antarctica had any effect on their sense of direction.

Iple couldn't understand why anyone in the team of scien-tists had come to Antarctica. He watched the rings get darker under their eyes. Asa the architect got so he was up for four hours and slept for one before he jittered back awake, not sure whether he had slept. To Iple, they all seemed to be haunting the igloos. Everyone made a lot of swooshing noise when they moved, with the rubbing of the weatherproof shells of their coats and pants, but somehow no one heard Iple. He would just be there suddenly, startling, in the peripheral view of a psy-chologist or a cosmologist or Asa or Tina or Roy the artificial intelligence man. It made Iple seem ominous. To Iple they seemed like nervous, frightened ghosts. He felt a little pity, and a little satisfaction at the chance that by not hearing himself, no one could hear him.

Nine. What Iple Found

As the days got longer, Iple stayed away longer. Sometimes, with the igloos still in view, he thought he could hear some hint of Penelope's flügelhorn; then when the igloos were gone, he relaxed his ears. He thought this might be what it was like to think straight, with all his senses feeling appropriate, and then he started to take unsystematic stock of his memories. He stayed out there, out past view of the village of igloos, sometimes for twenty hours at a time, misremembering his mother and father and their gestures and his siblings and childhood friends, if he'd had any, and the cars and the breakfasts and the lawns of his childhood, still hoping he might stumble across a real memory he could be sure of.

Then Iple saw a spot of red off in the distance. It must have been in his vision for a while before he noticed it. It wasn't far. It was Wes's parka, with Wes frozen into it, snow and ice caked deep into his beard and eyebrows and eyelashes. Iple was surprised to see Wes. Iple hadn't seen Wes leave his pile of blankets in the central igloo since they first laid him down there. Iple didn't think Wes was much inclined to move, and Iple especially didn't think Wes could make his way all this way away. Iple wanted to be proud of Wes for this unexpected gesture, but Wes was all frozen up and not breathing.

Iple figured this is what Wes had planned on when he set out from under his pile of blankets. He wasn't sure what to do with Wes. He was pretty sure Wes wasn't planning on getting found, and probably didn't want to be. Wes probably wanted to stay where he was. But then Wes probably also didn't have much of an idea now whether he'd been found or not. Iple tried to get a look out of Wes, maybe get a hint out of him, and Wes sat there with his eyes frozen shut. Iple pictured leaving

Wes there and Wes getting buried over by a few good gusts of snow. Iple could walk right past Wes tomorrow and not know it. It seemed lonely and wrong to Iple. He sat down and took his tea and half his sandwich, folded the other half into his coat, and hoisted Wes up over his shoulder.

Gradually Iple thought he could hear his feet crunching into the snow, and he tried not to think much of it. Then Wes spoke up.

"Is that you, Iple? You're taking me back to the ice-station?"

"I am taking you back to the ice-station," Iple said, his mouth almost too cold to articulate.

"Don't take me back there." Wes sounded good. His voice was calm and just a little amused. "You can drop me right here and I'll disappear right into the snow very quickly."

"What do you care where your body ends up?" Iple asked.

"And what do you care?"

"The knowledge of your presence will interfere with my enjoyment of the blankness of the landscape," said Iple.

"That's weird, Iple."

Iple reimagined the ice as dotted through with corpses, each one too cold to move, even just enough to give up its ghost.

"Please, Iple. Tina may cryonically reanimate me. It's something she's prepared for. She's eager to unfreeze someone. Don't make a failed suicide of me."

The roofs of the igloos crested over the horizon like angry swollen white bellies.

"There's something I'd like you to see, something exceptional," said Wes. "It's not terribly far. Let's at least stop there first." Iple didn't especially feel like going back to the village of igloos just yet. It was still early, and Wes sounded so benign and so minimally perturbed that Iple was curious. Wes talked Iple in the direction of the thing.

"You know what song I always loved?" Wes asked as Iple carried him. "I always loved 'Paper Moon.' It's so tenderly, beautifully solipsistic. And it's so casual, so effortlessly nonchalant;

every time I hear it, it comes like something very simple but elusive, almost animism; it's a love song to be sung by everything, by moon, sea, stone, ice, snow, wind. I always loved that song. Anyone can sing it, and it's always beautiful." Then Wes hummed it for a minute, and Iple thought he could feel Wes humming, and then Wes said, "Oh, this is it. Look down."

The ice was transparent under Iple's feet, so that, except for a little glare on the surface, it looked like he was floating. It was exceptional. And it went on like that, the giant piece of perfectly clear ice, and Iple could see, in the ice about thirty feet below him, a huge thing, on its back with its four legs all pointed straight up, like a cartoon of a huge dead thing.

Ten. Iple's Speech

Iple hadn't talked since the explosion had ruined his ears. He hadn't talked in anyone's presence. At first, he had been afraid to find out for sure that he couldn't even hear himself speak. He was also afraid that he might miraculously still be able to. After a week, he tried it. He tried reading a line aloud from the book he was reading up there in the janitor's attic. He knew the janitor was out.

"The explorers endured many hardships."

He might not have spoken it. He might have just moved his lips. He had to say it so he could feel his vocal cords move.

"The explorers endured many hardships."

Did he feel them move, or was that just breath wisping through his trachea in a lost whisper? He should at least be able to hear himself in some far away, underwater way.

"The explorers endured many hardships."

He felt the slight scrapes and pinches he used to feel at the top of his throat when he yelled.

"The explorers endured many hardships."

His throat burned a little, but still nothing, no far away, underwater voice.

"The explorers endured many hardships."

His throat felt raw. He went to get a glass of water to fix it. "Once more," he told himself.

Almost back to the village of igloos with Wes on his shoulder, he imagined he might soon have to say something. Always before he went to sleep, he exercised his mouth, tensed and flexed his lips, his tongue, his cheeks. For some time not moving his mouth except to eat felt strange, disturbingly calm, and once it felt natural, he started exercising his mouth before he went to sleep. He felt good about his conversation with Wes. He'd found himself very comprehensibly articulate.

Most everyone was in the kitchen igloo when Iple came in. "The madman's killed Wes!" shouted Asa the architect, grabbing a steak knife.

"Quiet, you infantile jackass," said Benjamin.

Iple spoke slowly. "I found Wes far from the ice-station, frozen. I believe he did not intend to return. I also found an enormous creature preserved in an uncanny bit of ice, not too far away."

Eleven. Iple's Afterlife

Iple got his hearing back. He got back senses he never knew he lost. He remembered things no one knows for sure, like that time is discrete and that our ways of measuring are awkward for the way the universe is. He remembered what his mother looked like. Very freckly. When he was two she went for a swim in the Mediterranean and never came back.

Iple's mother laughed at him for everything he'd forgotten and she told him that the thing with his memory, the thing with his ears, every awful thing, was just the kind of joke they all liked to play on each other. She'd been in on it all along, and now he was in on it, and now that it was over Iple agreed that it was funny. Then she said, "Now give me over your shoes, Iple."

Iple's shoes were soft brown leather. They were sturdy but forgiving. He'd had them repaired twelve times. They had been his favorite thing. "No shoes in the afterlife," she said, only she didn't call it the afterlife. Iple gave her over his shoes remorselessly, and she told him what else there wasn't. Wallpaper, clocks and watches, recorded music, nail polish . . .

Already he wasn't listening, but watching the breeze blow the hairs on her left freckled forearm.

Twelve. Asa

Iple had orange eyes. They looked fugitive. Iple liked to look around almost always, and it made Asa the architect, who never looked around unless he should, nervous. A few times Asa thought he saw Iple's eyes throw back light like a cat's. Asa came to Antarctica to see his dream of a village of igloos come true. Igloos connected by ice tunnels, and astonishingly warm inside, as if alive. It made Asa feel almost fetal to think of it.

Asa's wife didn't understand the village of igloos. They had two young boys, a beautiful home deep in the woods near Medicine Hat, and access to superlative fruits and vegetables. "Why are you going to Antarctica?" she asked Asa, and Asa couldn't very well answer.

"I want to build a snow fort," he thought.

Asa had trouble believing Iple couldn't hear. Asa thought Iple's eyes said he was listening. Iple would look over at the oven for a minute. "Now he is listening to the oven for a minute," Asa thought.

Asa worried over what Iple did away from the village of igloos. No one else ever left the village of igloos. They really were astonishingly warm inside, and everyone had a personal igloo, plus there was the common igloo, and the kitchen igloo, and down some long tunnels, but still comfortably warm, there were two outhouse igloos. They had gone ahead and used the auger, in terror and insistently. It hurt Asa that Iple didn't spend more time in his village of igloos, and that Iple never smiled at Asa, the way people always did in Medicine Hat and usually did in the village of igloos.

Benjamin also never smiled at Asa, and in fact once spat on Asa's boot and cursed Asa's imbecilic snow fort, but Benjamin did not make Asa nervous. Asa never heard Iple coming. Iple would be there all at once, and Asa would jump, first at the sudden appearance, and then again because it was Iple. Eventually he started jumping a third time, because his nerves had started to turn in on themselves, and sometimes a fourth.

Asa got so he drank a lot of coffee and lost control of his sleeping. He would sleep without knowing it, and sometimes be awake without knowing it, or fall asleep and dream a slight variation on just having been awake. He dreamt of his wife and boys, living in their beautiful home without him and not ever talking, he dreamt of Iple riding in on a brontosaurus and destroying the village of igloos, he dreamt of Iple riding through Medicine Hat, destroying his wife and boys, dashing their superlative produce, no one noticing until he was upon them, Iple, stealth annihilator, and then he woke up, not sure if he had slept.

Then Iple walked in with Wes on his shoulder like a sack of potatoes. For three days Asa wept into his coffee and wept while he was sleeping and dreamt of Iple carrying everyone, frozen, out of Medicine Hat, and whistling.

Iple really had started to whistle. He whistled the songs Penelope played on her flügelhorn, though he couldn't be sure he'd heard them, and he wasn't sure he was really whistling, but Penelope started to give him looks.

After three days of weeping, Asa crawled into Iple's igloo while Iple was sleeping and put a hole in Iple's throat with a penknife.

Thirteen. Life on Other Planets

There's a way by which things get unsorted. A crucial button takes a gyre-dive down the sink's drain. A language vanishes, turns to babble.

Iple feels better. He doesn't miss his favorite shoes. In the evenings he uses his brain like a crystal ball to watch over the living world. He enjoys now understanding languages, the Bantu languages, the Mandarin dialects, the dialects of the owl, the dialects of water. There's a brook Iple watches over, that tells all at once the many interlocking stories of its polliwogs.

There's a boy who looks like Iple did, who takes naps by the brook in the afternoon. He wakes up from these naps feeling right and calm, then goes back into the world to get unsorted.

When someone is taking a trip, one way to wish that person off is to say, "*in bocca al lupo*," which means, "travel in the mouth of the wolf." If the wolf's mouth will have you, it is the safest place to be. Just the world alone is so big that it's hard not to vaporize. But when traveling, there is also the giant emptiness between one place and the other to consider.

Fourteen. Iple and Benjamin

Before Asa opened a hole in Iple's throat in Iple's sleep, Benjamin went with Iple to where Iple had found the giant creature frozen in the ice. Benjamin was wearing snowshoes his father had given to him seventy-two years ago on Benjamin's seventeenth birthday. Benjamin's birthday was the fourth of February. On Benjamin's seventeenth birthday, he walked with his father through the snow drifts in his new snowshoes, and the father gave Benjamin some of his brandy to drink, and the snow came down in big compound flakes, slowly enough to study it as it fell, and Benjamin could not tell if his cheeks were very cold or very hot.

Now Benjamin carried an orange flag and a stainless steel hammer for tenderizing meat. The hood on his anorak zipped up to keep almost his whole face covered. His eyes stung and watered, but his cheeks stayed warm. Benjamin could hear a deep, hovering whistle all around him. He could see the horizon resonating to it. To ignore it he talked to Iple.

"I have never in all my days seen a sky as blank as the Antarctic sky. It's gone from the mind the instant one looks away from it. It's as forgettable as if it were nothing. Even at night, with the stars, if I look away and try to remember them, I remember different stars and not the ones I was looking at. You seem to like it well enough. Penelope tells me it's not so awful as I say it is.

"I don't know how much longer I am for this world, Iple." Benjamin took long pauses between each sentence to muster his breath, and it was a surprise to him when a sentence seemed to have come after the one before it.

"Iple, I have seen the way you look at Penelope. When she was five I learned the piano so I could teach it to her, you know. You must start early with these things. Music, languages, fine motor skills, reasoning powers. You must begin to establish the neural networks while the mind is still sufficiently adaptive. Her insights are now well beyond my own. She has grown into quite a beautiful young lady. I bought her flügelhorn, you know. When she was fourteen. I've seen the way you look at her, Iple. Everyone looks at her unusually, but you especially, because you don't notice yourself . . ."

Benjamin startled a little when Iple tugged at Benjamin's anorak sleeve and pointed into the clear ice.

"Good Christ, Iple, you've found a god-damned dinosaur."

Fifteen. Why Penelope Was a Microbiologist

When she was first just a little girl, Penelope liked chess. Then she liked other games, checkers and Parcheesi and Monopoly and Go and go fish and blackjack. She liked rules and made up rules and learned that some rules work better than others for making good games. She liked systems and she liked pure mathematics and the thought of big and little spheres gliding systematically through the universe. She liked to imagine the planets and quasars and pulsars and black holes as noble geniuses, who understood the rules of mathematics perfectly and obeyed because they were good sports. When that idea seemed too funny, she tried playing new games without making up the rules first, and tried to catch herself in the middle of the rules.

When Penelope learned to read, she liked to read detective stories. In detective stories the rules weren't mathematical enough to predict. Then she learned to predict the detective stories, and then she started to see all the rules. Then she read everything, and everything became a detective story. She just needed little clues for what might come next, and she got good at guessing right. Sometimes she was still surprised, and she liked to be surprised immensely.

Penelope started to wonder why she liked to be surprised so much. And so she became a detective looking for clues about where her brain came from, and so she looked at littler and littler things for answers, to find out where a thing stopped being just organized atoms and when it started being a thing capable of learning rules and being surprised, and then she tried to find a sign of pleasure at the surprise. Sometimes it seemed obvious to her that she would find out that even atoms get surprised and like it and that she should know that was the answer and that if she was reading a book about herself she would think that she herself was a too-slow detective and too careful not to get the wrong answer, maybe because she was too emotionally attached to the parties involved. That was something that sometimes happened to detectives.

Benjamin also wanted to know where his brain came from, but people always totally astonished him, and he could never guess at their rules and so he was a behaviorist psychologist. It amused him and also made him sad, but he was consoled by having taught Penelope how to play chess at such an early age, and by giving her detective books.

Sixteen. Zebedee's Day in Paris

Before he drove into the gas station, Zebedee was in Paris. He stood with his hands in the pockets of his camel-colored coat on the street corner. There was one cloud in the sky, and Zebedee watched a small hole open up in the cloud, and then he watched all the cloud's insides leak out through the hole.

Zebedee went to the goldbeater's shop, which smelled like lamb because the goldbeater ate a sandwich of lamb every day for lunch. A thief came into the goldbeater's shop once to steal the goldbeater's gold and the goldbeater took off one of the thief's ears. The goldbeater cleaned as much of the mess of blood as he could out of his shirtsleeves and out of his rug, and what he could not clean of the mess stayed there, and one day out of ten the goldbeater wore his shirt with bloodstains on the sleeves, and not even fools tried to steal from the goldbeater, and the goldbeater was a jovial, happy goldbeater full of lamb.

The goldbeater liked everyone, but especially Zebedee, because Zebedee has come in with gold that he had won gambling and said, "This gold is for you, and this other gold will you please hold onto, and sometimes I will come in needing a sheet of gold leaf," and Zebedee came in once or sometimes twice a year and they smiled to each other and said polite happy things to each other and the goldbeater gave Zebedee a sheet of gold leaf. And this time when Zebedee came into the goldbeater's shop Zebedee said how cloudlife will never cease to astonish him, and the goldbeater said how there was something that might interest Zebedee, that a man the goldbeater knew hoped to sell something Zebedee might like, and would Zebedee like to speak with the man, and Zebedee said certainly.

The man said, "I have a little xebec I like to take out in the spring and summer months."

"That's very nice," said Zebedee.

"I think so," the man said back, "but it has a figurehead, it's beautiful, somehow it doesn't wear in the water, I've always loved it, but now, I can't explain why, I feel the need to be rid of it, and when I mentioned it to the goldbeater, he thought of you immediately."

"Well, let's see it," said Zebedee. He looked up and saw that the insides of the cloud had spilled out so much that they were almost just more sky.

They went to the boat and Zebedee looked at the figurehead and it made his throat and nose constrict and he wept because he had expected to weep because he had expected the figurehead would be of a lady and look like Charlotte exactly as he remembered her, but it did not look like Charlotte but might have been her, or the figurehead might have been looking through this world and right at Charlotte. It was not the effect he was expecting, but it was a violent superstitious effect that made Zebedee weep. He bought the figurehead, and because he did not own much of anything else he had no address where he kept his things, and so he bought an address where he could keep the figurehead, and it stayed there alone in his house and he went to visit it at least once a month forever after that.

Seventeen. How They Got the Dinosaur Out of Antarctica

Benjamin used the meat-tenderizing mallet to hammer the orange flag into the ice where the dinosaur had been frozen into it. He looked at it for a long time. He looked at it and then looked away and then looked back. He looked away for a long time at a time, trying to imagine the ways his mind might have fooled him, and then looked back to see if his mind had fooled him one of those ways. He held his eyes closed until they didn't sting or water and looked back to see if this time it wasn't a dinosaur.

When Penelope was a girl she liked Benjamin to take her to the museum of natural history. Penelope liked the archaeologists because they were like detectives who weren't even sure what was the crime they were investigating, but still they were so careful, it was an implicit faith in criminality, in some high, hidden crime. So Benjamin saw the reconstructed dinosaur skeletons. He studied them lit by skylights from a bench while Penelope read each explanatory placard methodically and the museum of natural history made its murmur. He saw the plastic casts of the speculatively refleshed dinosaurs in their giant tropical diorama, and there was no mistaking this thing in the ice, it was a dinosaur. The ice was so smooth and clear it was like there was no ice. The eyes told the body it was floating to stand on it. Benjamin remembered buying his wife for their third anniversary a lily somehow at the center of a globe of glass, and he felt like a toy, or a pencil, something small and misplaced and only partially recollected.

Benjamin and Iple went back to the village of igloos and Benjamin said, "The boy found a god-damned dinosaur in the ice." The scientists talked about it and asked Benjamin if he was sure and he said Jesus yes he was goddamned sure.

They all went to bed and the next day had breakfast and packed lunches of tuna fish sandwiches and got bundled up and went out to where Benjamin had hammered the orange flag into the ice and they all looked at the dinosaur and looked at each other and at the dinosaur.

"It's a brontosaurus," said Penelope. "What a long tail."

Benjamin looked at the sky for an idea for ten minutes. "God damn this Antarctic sky," he said. The scientists stood around and ate their tuna fish sandwiches.

When they got back to the village of igloos Asa was unconscious in the common igloo with blood on his hands and arms and face, and Roy the artificial intelligence man found Iple in his bed.

Roy radioed to the government about Iple's murder and about the dinosaur, and all the scientists went home except for Benjamin, because Benjamin's brother was an ex-president. They built a brontosaurus laboratory at the edge of Patagonia and brought special helicopters to carry the brontosaurus in a big ice cube they cut and pulled right out of the continent. There were calculations. There were physicists, archaeologists, weathermen, public works administrators, helicopter repairmen, an ex-president and Eagle Scout, and a behaviorist psychologist.

Benjamin kept a radio in his igloo to talk to Penelope who was waiting in Argentina. "Tomorrow we're going to lift that thing right out of the continent. You should see all the ridiculous mechanisms they've got out here. It looks like we're getting ready to raise a circus tent over the whole Earth."

Eighteen. Penelope in Argentina

Penelope sat in a lawn chair and drank an iced tea with a thin wedge of lemon. The clouds arranged themselves into stacks and then leaned in a little toward Penelope. The ice chimed in her glass when she considered it, and the wind rustled the grass against itself. Penelope thought about microorganisms, about the minuscule things in the grass and the wind and the ice and the glass letting out many chiming roars, or atoms doing it, the atoms of the grass and the ice and the microorganisms, surprised again that they are atoms, chiming out, the electrons, almost weightless, vague and verging on nothingness, the very first hint of being, singing to themselves all alike, and singing too up and around and through her nerves, she the detective, if it was the electrons who did it, if they are willful, they will have a motive, and what is their motive.

The weather was so exactly fine it wasn't even weather. A young, bright, beautiful bird fell plum out of the sky and landed in Penelope's tea.

Nineteen. The Ex-President

The ex-president was seven years younger than Benjamin. Benjamin taught the ex-president how to tie his shoes. He taught him two ways to tie his shoes, and two ways to double-knot them, and how to quickly untie a double-knot. Benjamin taught the ex-president everything the ex-president knows about slipknots. He taught him stickball. He taught him how to hold the stick and how to step when he swung and how to drop the stick and run. He taught him how to slide into the second baseman to break up a double play and how to consider the wind on a long throw. He taught him how to whistle and how to whistle with his pinkies in the corners of his mouth and how to whistle through a blade of grass. Benjamin taught the ex-president how to steal an apple and how to smoke a cigar and how to drink wine. He taught him how to take gasoline out of a car without drinking it and how to expect bad weather. He taught him how to throw a rock through a window and how to pick a lock. He taught him how to ride a cow. He taught him how to fall off a roof. He taught him how to sweet-talk girls and how to sweet-talk boys and how only to do it if he had to. He taught him how to palm anything smaller than his palm and how to keep it inconspicuously palmed. He taught him when to let his mind wander. He taught him how to take off an orange peel in one piece. He taught him how to snap. He taught him how to catch a bird and pluck it and make a fire and cook it. He taught him how to skin. He taught him how to hide. He taught him how to mail a letter. He taught him how to kill a man with one punch and how to unfold a butterfly knife and how to shoot and how to aim and how to make a Molotov cocktail and how to throw it. Benjamin taught the ex-president how to shut up and how to tell what a person wants more than anything else. He taught him how to hold a snake.

The ex-president had green irises and small pupils. He had hair that nobody had a name for what color it was. He played minor league baseball. He taught himself how to ride a train and how to jump on a moving train. He taught himself how to kiss and how to make a martini and how to make a Manhattan. He taught himself how to write newspaper articles. He taught himself how to look at a train wreck and turn it into a newspaper article. He taught himself how to dance fast and how to dance slow. He taught himself how to go to a war with no gun, with nothing but a pencil and a notebook and a helmet, and turn it into a newspaper article or a magazine feature and live. He taught himself how to ride a boat but not how to ride an airplane. He had the most nieces and nephews of any ex-president. Everyone loved him when he was president. He got rid of the spaceships but not the great telescopes. And even the astronauts loved him, though they had nothing left but to go swimming and raise their children.

Twenty. Where They Took the Dinosaur

The ex-president was a master of secrecy. When he was president, there was a prince, and the prince wanted to kill the president. The president starved the prince to death, and not even the prince knew who had starved him. The ex-president liked to keep things secret just for fun, but he also thought there might be a good reason to keep the frozen dinosaur a secret. No cameras came to Antarctica to help move the dinosaur to Argentina. And instead of building a dinosaur laboratory in Argentina, the ex-president built a self-powered baseball stadium, with solar panels and windmills, and underneath the baseball stadium he built a dinosaur laboratory.

He put together a team of Argentineans with an acrobat shortstop. The shortstop had the goldbeater for an uncle. He had his uncle's copper-colored irises and a matching beard. He played like he had the baseball on a string around his finger. He played with no glove, and he threw with either arm. Dancers came to watch him play, with the lithe arms of the windmills turning in the sky out beyond the outfield.

Tina the doctor came and rode down the giant cargo elevator. The ex-president had them make a giant cargo elevator so they could sneak in the dinosaur. There were other huge things in the dinosaur laboratory. Huge climate control devices. When Tina got down there it was still very cold because they weren't ready just yet to unfreeze the dinosaur. She put on her mittens.

The dinosaur sat there suspended in its enormous ice-cube, and the ice-cube was covered over with a big purple drape. The ceiling in the dinosaur laboratory was two times as high as the enormous ice-cube. There was nothing in the dinosaur laboratory really except the giant ice-cube and the purple drape and Tina and the ex-president. The floor was made of cement and it had a little drain-hole in it. Then there was a door and a big window and on the other side of the window was where they kept all the devices. They kept two fancy computers, and a centrifuge, and a few optical microscopes, and a special neutron microscope, and some Petri dishes. They had some Persian rugs that Benjamin had brought down because he liked to walk on them in his bare feet. Before he could bring them down, Benjamin had to have the rugs thoroughly beaten. Then he had to have them irradiated so that no dangerous little thing could live in them. Benjamin enjoyed having his rugs irradiated. He pretended to be very serious about it.

They called the room with the dinosaur "the dinosaur room," and they called the room with all the devices "the devices room." They came and went through the devices room, up and down a long spiral staircase. Benjamin and the ex-president both thought the stairs would make for good exercise. But the ex-president liked to bring people down on the huge cargo elevator if the people were coming down for the first time. He thought it was dramatic, and he liked to do dramatic things for people.

While Tina was looking at the giant ice-cube under its drape, the ex-president talked to her about security, about how they would be watching her carefully, but how they also had to trust her, and how he didn't mind trusting her. Then he talked to her about how he didn't like to kill people, but that sometimes people made it so he had to do that, and it annoyed him. He said that what really annoyed him was that usually he had even warned the people beforehand not to make him have to do it, but that they went ahead and didn't listen to him. And that just really annoyed him, because usually they were people that he liked, and he wished that the people he liked would just be sensible enough to listen to him. So he said to Tina, "Tina, I like you, and I am going to have to trust you, and I don't mind trusting you. I am trusting you with this secret. It is a secret. Now, can you keep it a secret?"

Tina kept looking at the big ice-cube and nodded. Then she looked at the ex-president and nodded again, and then she made a little smile. The ex-president said OK, and led the way to the devices room. Tina thought there was something about the ex-president that was cute.

Twenty-one. A Little Bit About Tina

Tina liked to cut her own hair. She had a pair of big orange-handled scissors she had bought at a stationery store that she used for everything. She used the orange-handled scissors to open envelopes and taped-up cardboard boxes and the foil seals on jars of peanut butter and packets of powder for macaroni and cheese. She cut her old bluejeans into shorts with them. When she couldn't tie the knot out of her shoelace, she used the orange-handled scissors to cut the knot out. She used them to cut the grass where the lawn mower couldn't reach, like around the swingset, and she used them to cut her hair. She didn't look in the mirror when she cut her hair. She went into the bathroom and turned the light off and took off her clothes and cut her hair in the dark. She cut her hair short, and she cut it about every three months, and standing there with her hair in her right hand and the orange-handled scissors in her left hand, and the sound of the hairs being scissored, and the scissored hairs brushing her shoulders, it was something sacrosanct to her.

Tina was left-handed, and so her pair of orange-handled scissors was left-handed. She packed them with her on vacations. She packed them with her when she went to the village of igloos. After Wes took off his arm, she used the orange-handled scissors to cut his shirt off.

Tina knows as much about cryobiology as almost anyone. Before she went to the village of igloos, she had been freezing all kinds of animals and bringing them back to life. She froze mice and chinchillas and rabbits and dogs, a prairie dog, a pig, but especially she froze monkeys and baboons and gorillas and chimpanzees and an orangutan. She got so no one could tell the difference between a monkey she had frozen and a monkey she hadn't frozen. If you don't freeze and unfreeze the monkey just right, it goes a little funny after it's unfrozen. She called it daydreaming. "Ever since Lena thawed," she would tell her mother, "she's been prone to daydreaming." But Tina had become a cryobiological virtuoso. Her monkeys' eyes stayed bright after they thawed, and they daydreamed no more than ordinary monkeys.

At the village of igloos, she froze animals just out in the cold. She would just leave a guinea pig outside the door in an open shoebox. The animals she froze and unfroze at the village of igloos had come out relatively bright-eyed. But she had not been able to unfreeze Wes. And she had never frozen anything bigger than a gorilla. She told the ex-president she couldn't be sure about the dinosaur. The ex-president got her an elephant to practice on, and the elephant did thaw very nicely. She told the ex-president that she thought there was a good chance for the dinosaur, and that she had high hopes.

Twenty-two. Penelope at Her Microscope

Benjamin bought Penelope her first microscope when she was twelve. She cracked five slides in a row by focusing the lens down on them, and each time it made her jump. Then she got it to focus, and spent a week staring at all of a glass of pondwater. It was summertime, and Penelope's mother convinced her to stare into the microscope out on the porch. She ate peanut butter and jelly sandwiches and carrot sticks and stared into the microscope. She stared at jelly through the microscope, and then she stared at peanut butter. She took a fly from the windowsill and took it apart with a pair of fingernail clippers and stared at it. She cut a thin slice of carrot with a razor and stared at it. She learned how to slice a very thin slice of anything. She learned how to shave a blade of grass.

Now Penelope was looking at a slide of dinosaur blood through the microscope. Now when she touched the microscope, she barely touched it. She touched it like it just needed a hint from her of what to do and then it would do that thing. She stared into the microscope at the dinosaur blood and it looked just like ordinary people blood. Penelope looked all day for something that made the blood look different than ordinary blood. Then she ate a coffee bean and drank a glass of water.

Twenty-three. The Shortstop

Everyone loved the Argentinean shortstop who played in the stadium up above the dinosaur laboratory. Everyone loved him so much that they never bothered him for his autograph or to stop and have a picture taken or even to tell him how much they loved him. They just smiled and nodded or said hello or tipped their hats or made like they were tipping an imaginary hat, or sometimes the ladies with skirts curtsied or they curtsied with imaginary skirts or else they pretended not even to notice him because they loved him so much, and then when he left, they said, "That was the shortstop," or once in a while someone asked how he was and he would say, "I'm fine, thank you."

The shortstop was superstitious and could only ever say, "I'm fine, thank you," if someone asked how he was. He had grapefruit juice every morning. Every night when he left the stadium he went to the vegetable stand and bought four grape-fruits to squeeze into a glass of grapefruit juice the next morn-ing. The fruit and vegetable stand had been open by accident the first night the shortstop came to it, and now it stayed open every night until he came for his grapefruits. Some nights the fruit and vegetable man would go home to his family and leave the four grapefruits there in a crate. Every morning the short-stop squeezed himself a glass of grapefruit juice and before he drank it, he licked the juiced grapefruit skins and threw them out his window into the tall grass. Then he pulled a hair from his head and drank it in his grapefruit juice. He tapped every doorhandle before he turned it. He shook every sock twice before he put it on. He came home at lunchtime every day and fluffed his pillow. He took two deep breaths between when he thought a new thought and when he said it. He waited every night until the stadium was empty, and then he went onto the field and lay down in the dark, dense outfield grass, and felt the earth getting colder, and the sky drawing out the warmth of the earth, and then he drew a blankness over his senses, until he started to feel a shiver from the center of the earth. Really it was the shiver of the huge climate control devices in the dinosaur laboratory, but the shortstop listened to it carefully, until he felt himself click open like a lock. Then he left to get his grapefruits.

Twenty-four. They Go Ahead and Unfreeze the Dinosaur

There was only so much they could do with a frozen dinosaur. First they unfroze her surrounding ice-cube. Then she was just standing there in the dinosaur room, just like a real dinosaur, only frozen. She was a beautiful brontosaurus, and not just because she was the only one left and she was frozen like a monument and because just about everything is beautiful when it's frozen. No, even when there were dinosaurs every-where, and all kinds of beautiful ones, like the stegosaurus with its twin rows of plates like a stern, intent plumage down its spine, even then the brontosaurus was the most beautiful dinosaur, because of its slight, far-away head, and its little over-bite, and the suede-soft skin of its neck and belly. When the other dinosaurs decided to kill a brontosaurus, they wept for it and kept quiet around each other until it was time, and after-ward they kept quiet too and some continued to weep after, and they slept badly for the beautiful thing they ate, and even for a brontosaurus, frozen or not frozen, she was a beautiful brontosaurus, standing still in the dinosaur room. Tina want-ed to paste some nice thick eyelashes on her.

Instead, she took a few chromosomes off the dinosaur's beautiful shank, so that Penelope can look at its deoxyribonu-cleotides. And that was it. There was nothing else to do but unfreeze it. The ex-president thought it was awfully sudden. He was used to things taking time, especially special things like this. But oh well.

"Oh, well," said the ex-president. He rubbed his chin. Then he crossed his arms. Then he bowed. Then he sighed and looked around. Then he said, "Alright, let's go ahead then," and then they went ahead and unfroze that big beauti-ful dinosaur, and even that took hardly any time.

They stood in the devices room and watched through the window that looked into the dinosaur room, and the dinosaur just seemed to slowly sink down, slowly and gently and dreamily down onto the floor, like she was just very carefully laying herself down for a nap. Tina thought the dinosaur might look good with a nightcap. She also thought to herself, "That is not an alive dinosaur."

When she had unfrozen the elephant, it just went ahead and took a little stroll around the laboratory. Now the brontosaurus was lying on the floor, limp like a miraculous beanbag. The ex-president and Benjamin and Penelope all looked at the dinosaur lying there and thought that it was not an alive dinosaur. Benjamin rubbed the bottoms of his bare feet on his irradiated Persian rug.

The brontosaurus lay there and had a long, complicated fantastic dream. She dreamt her name. At first her name was so faint in the dream it was as if a bumblebee were telling it to her. A bumblebee with its mouth full. But even then she knew it was her name coming back to her and she just kept dreaming and waited for her name to resolve itself and it came closer, until she could hold it in the periphery of her dreaming, and she felt how it was to hold it, so she held it closer, until she recognized it, and then she recognized more of it, and she remembered its secrets, its worn-away places, its tricks, and how to internalize it, and she dreamt whether or not she should go ahead and internalize it, and she remembered herself, and how she did being she with her name, and she tried remembering a different name for herself, but no, this was her irresistible name and she loved it and she dreamt it back to herself, and she called to herself, "'Lo, Isabella," and she answered herself, "Yes, Isabella."

Isabella's dream took her a week to dream. The ex-president took a nap that week and dreamt his own name. He dreamt himself flirting and dancing a tango, saying, "Please, call me Harry." The lady smiled and blushed and looked to the floor. He knew she couldn't do it, she could not call him

Harry, and his face felt heavy with wanting to weep. She was Valentina Vladmirovna Tereshkova, the first woman in space.

Twenty-five. Penelope's Discovery

One of the things Penelope knew how to do was look at genes. Like I said before, Penelope thought of herself as a detective, and so the genes were always an obvious and reliable clue, but one that only ever answered questions tangential to her central mystery. They bored her a little. She wished for a more exotic clue, like for a screw from the dead man's eyeglasses to appear in her minestrone, or to discover the chauffeur hides a scimitar under his mattress.

Penelope has a whole process for looking at genes, and it takes a lot of busywork around her laboratory, with centrifuges and test tubes and what-all, and while she spun the centrifuge she considered that any person might only do one or two great things in a life, or that every person might do one or two great things in a life, and they might be the wrong things, an accident or an unconscious gesture. Penelope thought about her great-uncle Harry the ex-president. Harry had a boy named Louis and Louis was bright and always woke up at 5:30 in the morning and brushed his teeth and played a game of chess with himself, and he could make people relax without their noticing. He never spoke quickly. His eyes almost never looked like they looked at a thing, and in the evening he came home and put on music and danced around the living room. Sometimes he brought home someone to dance with, a girl from school, or the lady from the drugstore, still wearing her apron and her name tag, or Penelope, when she was four or five, he danced with her on his knees.

Then one morning Harry had a funny feeling and went and told Louis not to go to school that day because it must be a zero humidity day, the air just felt right to breathe, and he gave Louis a few subway tokens and a rub on the head, and Louis smiled and looked not quite at Harry and said, "Oh well. Alright," and went out and disappeared, and somehow this was the great thing the ex-president had done in his life.

The centrifuge beeped and stopped and Penelope took the dinosaur genes out and worked on them some more. When she could finally get a good look at them, they were all wrong. They were one hundred times bigger than ordinary people genes.

Twenty-six. Interviews with the Shortstop

The shortstop was especially gifted at giving interviews. He answered each question slowly, making sure not to break his answers on their way out. He imagined that with each one he was formulating a magnificently fragile teacup that he might hand to a reporter. Even though the reporters only ever asked him the same question again and again. They asked him how he had done what he had done that day.

But every time, he considered the question, and very rarely did his answers resemble one another. One time he tells the reporters, "My mother had no money for toys, so my only toy was a baseball that had crashed through our kitchen window on the day I was brought back from the hospital. Right away, my brothers tried to steal it from me. So I learned quickly how to keep it. I could not be cautious and huddle over it, because I had many brothers and they would overpower me. So I became adventurous. I got comfortable with getting attacked for my ball. I looked forward to it. I learned how to trick my brothers into noticing me when they should be noticing the ball, and noticing the ball when they should be noticing me, and once they weren't noticing me, I would do something to surprise them. I thought it might help if I could learn to surprise even the ball. But the ball cannot be surprised. At least, I cannot surprise it. I believe it notices everything."

Another time he says, "I do not know if what I do is so superlative. Today the bat boy did some extraordinary things that none of you noticed."

Another time, "I make an inordinate number of mistakes when I am not playing the game. I drop precious things. I offend strangers. I am lost for hours at a time. This way, I am not anxious to make mistakes on the field. I have trouble deciding whether this is a better life, whether I might not prefer to make fewer mistakes in the world and no longer play as a shortstop. But I feel as though I must continue before I can be sure."

Once a reporter seemed very angry with him and asked him, almost scornfully, "What makes you think you can just do the things you've been doing out there?"

The other reporters let out stifled discomforted laughs, but the shortstop stayed serious, and he said, "I am never entirely sure that I can do these things."

On the evening Isabella had been thawed in the laboratory underneath the stadium, a reporter said to him, "You turned that triple play in the third before the runners or even the umpires knew what was happening. How were you able to even think that quickly?"

The shortstop answered, "I suspect at times that I am listening to a voice that has been secretly sewn into the atmosphere, and that my ear is pinned to one of the stitches that keeps this voice mostly hidden. I am listening to it, but I can not hear it enough to be sure that it exists as a sound, or that there is any actual sewing involved."

The shortstop answered the question and answered the question. After one very exhausting answer, he got up and said politely, "I am sorry, gentlemen and gentlewomen, I do not know how many more times I will be able to answer your question."

Twenty-seven. Iple's Knife

Knives weren't allowed in the afterlife, but Iple had snuck one in, a beautiful, heavy butterfly knife, which he twirled about distractedly in his hand like a majorette, twirling it open, twirling it closed, twirling it open . . .

Iple had taken the time to learn a trick with the butterfly knife, and he liked to use the trick when he was just first meeting someone. They would introduce each other, and at the first conversational lull, Iple would show the new person his butterfly knife. Most of the time, as soon as he opened his hand to show the knife there in his palm, the new person would first startle, and sometimes say, "Where did you get a knife? There are supposed to be no knives here." Then the new person would make a move to confiscate Iple's knife, to turn it over to the appropriate authorities. Very few people in the afterlife approved even the mildest gestures of sedition.

But at the moment that the new person moved as if to take the knife, Iple held up his finger, took a step back, and arched his eyebrows, as if to say, "I understand your alarm, but if you will be patient, I will demonstrate that this is actually a quite benign object. After all, I am not a monster. Do I look like a monster?" These movements of Iple's never failed to quiet his new acquaintance's fears, at least provisionally.

Next, Iple clasped his hands together, with the knife between them, and worried his hands against one another, as if worrying the knife inside his hands. Then he held his hand out once again. The knife was still there, unchanged. He looked at the new person looking at the knife. The new person inevitably looked up into his orange eyes. Then Iple looked back down at the knife, as if instructing the new person to join him in looking at it. And then, right there under the new person's watching, the butterfly knife would mutate into an actual butterfly. It just mutated. You could see it happening. And then Iple would make a nod of his head, gesturing to the butterfly to fly off, and the butterfly would go and fly off. This trick never failed to delight a new acquaintance.

But the greatest part of his trick Iple never showed, which was that the butterfly knife was still right there enjoying itself in his palm, waiting until the new person went on his or her way, that he might twirl it open again, twirl it closed again, open, closed . . . his trusty, forbidden knife, twirling through the air, which actually was very heaven-like.

Twenty-eight. Isabella in the Laboratory

When Isabella woke from her name-dream, Tina was there giving Isabella an injection. When they all figured out that the unfrozen Isabella was very much an alive dinosaur, it was a big surprise. Before they had figured it out, Isabella had looked too hopelessly unalive to believe. Benjamin had said, "That is one fantastically costly prehistoric lump of death." Harry, the ex-president, said nothing.

Tina was fearful. She felt like she was holding a mouthful of razor blades. She managed to get out, "Let me just take a look," and she ran into the dinosaur room. Right away she felt a little better, lighter. When she got close to Isabella, she could feel how the life was running through her, roughly at first, then, more smoothly, and more smoothly, until the life was running evenly throughout Isabella. Tina liked to hold her breath so she could feel a little of that feeling when she let her breath start up again, that feeling of her life resmoothening.

Isabella still looked like an inert pile from the devices room, but from here Tina could feel her running like a giant, brilliant machine.

"We have an alive dinosaur," she called.

When Isabella kept not waking up, Tina started in with a series of injections, and everyone waited and hoped and the ex-president asked himself, how long would he be waiting here with a comatose brontosaurus, and then, while Tina was giving her another injection, Isabella woke up.

She was drowsy and calm and happy from her dream, and nothing alarmed her about Tina there with a needle in Isabella's leg, and nothing about the dinosaur room in general alarmed her, and by the time she was aware enough to possibly be alarmed, it felt to Isabella like it was too late to fuss. But

Isabella had not ever fussed once. Isabella's mother had always said that Isabella had a calm soul.

"When Isabella was born, she took two big blinks, and she looked all around, and then she just looked at me and smiled like we were old friends. She didn't make a sound," her mother had always said.

Twenty-nine. Good-bye to Tina

Once Isabella woke up, it was the end of Tina's role in the dinosaur project. Tina had done a very good job unfreezing the dinosaur. It had been suspenseful, for which Benjamin thanked her. He said he liked it much better that everything had been so suspenseful, and that they would make a special bank account for her and put money in it for her at regular intervals, and not to forget her conversation with the ex-president about the importance of keeping everything secret. Then he poured her a glass of champagne to celebrate her departure.

Tina went home and gave up cryobiology. Tina's mother asked her why all of a sudden was she giving up cryobiology, after all Tina loved cryobiology so much.

"Oh," Tina said to her mother, "You start to feel like you're just thawing the same poor mouse over and over again."

"But what about that elephant you did?" asked her mother. "I thought that was really spectacular. You know, I've gotten to really enjoy telling people about what you do."

The ex-president did consider putting Tina in the way of an accident, so she might not accidentally tell a journalist or a spy about the dinosaur. As a younger man, as the President, he certainly would have, but now he felt too light-hearted. So he just kept putting money in her bank account and lost track of her.

The last he checked, she had made a little darkroom in her basement, and she was taking pictures of her house. She might rearrange a room ten or twelve times in a day to take pictures of it each way. She might move all the furniture into the yard, or roll her couch through the snow, and take many pictures of it. She might rent a helicopter to hover there over her house while she takes pictures. She might put all the rugs up there on the roof to take pictures of them from the neighbor's roof.

Eventually she gave up photography, too, and soon after that everyone lost track of her. No one is sure if she met with a sudden accident, or a long, drawn-out accident, and that was the end of her, or if she jumped into the ocean, and that was the end of her, or if she went and cryonized herself, so she might later get yet another angle from which to shoot her house.

Thirty. Isabella's Thoughts on Coming Back to Life

Isabella was not so confused about what had happened to her body. She was not under the impression that she might simply be waking up from a routine afternoon nap. She made an effort to access her most recent memories, and those were her memories of walking around in deep cold and thinking how soon she would freeze. She remembered her long swim to Antarctica, and she smiled at the thought of it. Isabella had not had a nice, quiet, peaceful moment to think fondly about her triumphant swim. The other dinosaurs had all known Isabella had a gift for swimming, but none of them would have believed she could make such a long swim through that thick, freezing water.

It was nice and quiet and peaceful in the dinosaur room at the dinosaur laboratory. They brought Isabella nice piles of leaves, and they took away her manures, and otherwise they left her pretty well alone, to stroll, or to lie down, or to sit with her legs tucked under her like a camel and meditate.

When Isabella froze, her brain shut down almost as soon as the rest of her body did. She didn't have any conscious thoughts, and she didn't have any unconscious thoughts, either. But something else kept alive inside her, some tiny resilient thing that would have been happy to leave her body, except that she was frozen, so it couldn't leave, and now that she was unfrozen and her brain and her body were working again, the thing was happy enough to stay there inside her. It was secretly fond of living there inside the functional Isabella, though technically it was supposed to have no preference as to where it went, but it could not help itself; Isabella charmed it.

And this thing could remember perfectly well how long Isabella had been frozen, and it let her know how long she had been frozen in its quiet, subtle way, so that Isabella felt like she herself remembered it, and this was how she could tell she was not just waking up from an ordinary afternoon nap, but from thousands of years of her body being shut down. The climate control devices in the dinosaur room kept it nice and warm, and Isabella felt like she was safely at the end of her very difficult travels.

People were not such a baffling thing for Isabella to see. She could still remember the faces of her great, ancient ancestors, who were people. She could still remember many of the events, even the merely ordinary events, of their great, ancient lives.

Thirty-one. Isabella's Mnemonic Device

Isabella had an exceptional memory, and it survived her long hibernation in the ice with no omissions. It came back to her casually, as though it hadn't been away. She couldn't say she had missed it or noticed it missing. Her memory was tied to her name, and when she dreamt her name back into herself, her memory slipped back into her with it. She considered that her name might be a kind of password back into herself. And now here were all her memories back with her, whole and obedient.

She remembered her swim to Antarctica, and she remembered each of her six thousand twenty other swims, her great swim down the Yangtze into the East China Sea, her everyday twilight swims in the Mediterranean as a girl, her swims up the insides of tsunami waves, tossing her like a pale piece of ribbon, the long solitary swims of her emigrations, of which the swim to Antarctica had been the last, and her leisure swims, her mere wades, her floats. A brontosaurus is born already remembering how to swim.

Isabella remembered the number six thousand twenty not as a tally or a figure, but as a thing grasped all at once, the way a person grasps the number two right away, seeing two fingers. If a dinosaur is to think of any number, the dinosaur must think of it all at once, because dinosaurs have no hands to write with and no way to turn a number from a number into writing, to be considered later and estimated back into a number, the way a person might do. And so dinosaurs have a special skill for knowing very big numbers all at once, especially numbers that come slowly, the way Isabella's number of swims had come to her, across her whole life.

And on each swim, Isabella would consider her other swims, to learn over again how any one thing is at once different from any other thing and at the same time common to other things. During one wading session, seventeen flies landed on Isabella's back at once. Flies had landed on her back before, and she thought of these other times, and the other times she simply waded, and the times when the sun was the same warmth as now, and the times when her head was perfectly warm from the sun and her feet were perfectly cold in the water, as now, and yet never before had seventeen flies landed on her back at once. Isabella made a careful practice of learning to recognize similarity and difference. It was something a brontosaurus just did naturally. Isabella's mother had done the same. Each memory, then, was distinctly catalogued, with the appropriate cross-references to other memories.

Isabella kept up a complex memory, but it was something she believed was worth keeping. She supposed it helped her to make herself happier and less bewitched by a world which she felt was out to utterly stupefy her. Though at times she wondered if it might be not the world, but her own heavy memory, trying to trick her. She could remember the stars exactly, through every season and every hemisphere, and which ones were wandering where through the sky, and by how many fractions of a degree every ten years, and which were the first to get shone out as the moon got brighter. She noticed immediately when one was lit or snuffed.

She remembered the network of veins in each fern leaf, and the habits of dew and raindrops that might settle in the veins, and the way an insect might drink the dew or the rain, and which insects preferred dew to rain or rain to dew. She kept an inventory of crippled insects, and a subordinate inventory of insects missing wings, and whether one or both wings, and if one, which. She remembered the clouds and each of the many things each cloud resembled and to what degree it resembled each one and how so. Most of all the clouds resembled previous clouds. She remembered her mother and her mother's eyes and eyelids and cheekbones and the corners of her mother's mouth, which could turn in every direction, sometimes independently of each other. She remembered her mother's chin. She remembered the glimpses she'd caught of the inside of her mother's mouth, which was not at all pink like the inside of Isabella's mouth or most mouths, but a dark gray, almost black.

She remembered her mother's turns of speech, and how they had changed over time, how her mother almost entirely stopped saying "so to speak," which she'd used to say sometimes twice a sentence, by the time Isabella was one year old.

She remembered her time in the egg, the pink, speckled light that made its way through the eggshell and the warm, sweet, crisp smell of her own quick breaths, her tail curled up over her belly, her neck bowed down to where her chin rested against the sole of her right hind foot.

Thirty-two. More About Isabella's Mnemonic Device

Isabella could remember the moment her body intuitively flexed itself out of its egg, how all her muscles all at once had cringed, and then uncringed, and then she was in the dry open air, with its gentler smell and whiter light. She could remember her mother standing there over her, making a shadow for Isabella to stand in, and looking up at her mother's far-off head. Isabella felt her eyes drying out in this new outside air, and she blinked. Her mother's head was still indistinct. She blinked again.

Isabella could remember even before she was born. She remembers her mother laying the egg with Isabella inside. Her mother was looking off distractedly at a pterodactyl perched and bobbing on the branch of a fig tree. Isabella could remember the itch her mother was feeling on the inside of her nose exactly as she was laying Isabella's egg. She remembered the itch, and the pterodactyl, and each fig on the fig tree, exactly as her mother had remembered them. She remembered when her mother met her father, her father sneaking up on her mother, a hard trick for a brontosaurus, especially for her father, who'd had a sharp piece of stone stuck in his foot since he was a boy. Isabella remembered when he stepped on that stone, chasing a giant moth, and how it stung his foot with every step he took after that.

Isabella remembered what her grandparents remembered, and her great grandparents and so on. Ancestors who never met in their actual lives met in Isabella's memories. Isabella's inherited memories were as natural to her as the ones she built with her own senses. That was the way a dinosaur memory worked, and Isabella could remember far enough back to remember why. She remembered her great great ancient ancestors' conversations, back when dinosaurs were something utterly new and there hardly was any such thing as a dinosaur memory.

"Yesterday I called Amy a lachrymose ignoramus," Isabella can remember her great great ancestor Noel saying. "I feel rather awful about it. Do you suppose there's any way to keep that memory from passing on to my little brontosaur?"

Ping, a very clever stegosaurus, considers Noel's question. He reflexively stomps with one front foot while he's thinking, like a horse counting. It's something even some of the stegosaurs from Isabella's age couldn't help themselves from doing. After a good bout of stomping, Ping looks at Noel and says, "I don't think so, Noel. From what I understand, they'll remember anything you remember. And I, for one, have had a very difficult time forgetting much of anything."

"I've found the same," says Noel. "The people have no trouble forgetting even the simplest things. They make jokes about it. I have found myself completely unable to forget. Amy was quite stunned with me yesterday. I made her collapse completely. It was a terrible thing to watch. That's something I don't want to pass along, Ping."

"I'm afraid it's everything or nothing. You have the consolation of knowing that the child will also remember your regrets, yes? Your consciousness, taken altogether, the child will gain from it and love you for it. And who knows? Perhaps there can be no such thing as inherited memories. The people seem certain enough, but the people are forgetful. We shall see. Perhaps only some memories will be inherited, perhaps none will be. Perhaps the memories will degenerate from one generation to the next. Perhaps in three or four generations, you will be only a vague notion in anyone's memory, with the rougher moments smoothed out."

The memories did not degenerate. Isabella remembered Amy's look when Noel called her a lachrymose ignoramus, and she remembered how Amy had felt from it, like her belly had been split open and her throat pulled through it, since Amy too was Isabella's great great ancestor and so Isabella remembered everything that was Amy's. It was not such an awful memory as Noel worried it might be, but the early generations worried a lot about how their memories would be remembered, since after all it was such a new thing.

But the memories did not degenerate, not at all; they were passed down just as true and clear as they had been the moment they were committed to memory, though of course no one could be absolutely sure, but they felt that way, and it was true, they were that way, passed along and along, perfectly purely, again and again. They did not degenerate, even when everything else about the dinosaurs degenerated and they started being born all wrong and already dying, even then their quick lives were replete with a brilliant archive of remembrances.

Thirty-three. Isabella's First Impossible Memory

An extraordinary amount of dinosaur thought was preserved from one generation to the next, and still an extraordinary amount disappeared. Memories were passed down physically, in the genes, like eye color and reflex speed. A dinosaur passed down only the memories it had made before making its child. There were no first-hand memories of dying anywhere in all the dinosaur genes, although they had tried. The early ones had tried to make children between themselves and the newly dead, in hopes of recovering the elusive last memories and the sublime memories of the next world. At least, they imagined they were sublime, or felt that they must know whether they were sublime or not, or if it wasn't exactly necessary to know, it was at least a rare and interesting chance. But it never worked, and after a few generations everyone gave up on trying to capture any memories beyond memory, which is how they all had begun to think of death, and how they gave each other news of someone's dying. "Horace has gone beyond memory." For the dinosaurs this idea became at once a simple truth and a kind of consolation and sympathy.

But somehow Isabella had caught a memory of her mother's from after her mother had made her. Isabella remembered her mother chewing on a branch from a pomegranate tree, and the sweet pucker of its seeds, when her mother looked over to see Isabella hatch, and Isabella can remember her mother looking at Isabella and thinking that now she could think what she pleased and Isabella wouldn't know, that her memories were her own again, that her little spy had hatched and its awful work was done, and then she braced herself for Isabella to cry. She winced and waited there, the chewed pomegranate branch going spongy in her mouth. Already Isabella could tell she was having very inappropriate memories, and a corner of her mind grew deeply worried, and the rest of her worked to hide the problem from her mother. She stayed calm. She smiled at her mother and blinked. Her mother relaxed a little. She blinked again. Yes, now her mother was really feeling fine. Isabella could tell that soon she would stop having her mother's memories altogether.

Thirty-four. The Shortstop Notices Something Unusual

It was still the middle of the season when Isabella's big memory lurched back into motion, and almost every night, and sometimes also in the afternoon, they played a game in the baseball stadium above the dinosaur laboratory.

The stadium was shaped more like an ellipse than like a baseball stadium. The ex-president said he did it that way because he had loved the old Polo Grounds. Really it had been an accident. He had just forgotten, when he drew up the plans, what a baseball stadium was shaped like.

For every game, the stadium filled up with people. The American teams and the Japanese teams and the Cuban teams all made special trips to play against the Argentines. A German carmaker put together a team especially to come and play against the Argentines. They stayed for a week and played twelve games. By the end of the week, the German team had three hits and scored one run, when the Argentine catcher actually fell asleep with the ball in his glove after catching a fastball. When the umpire woke up the catcher and told him what had happened, he laughed and shrugged and waved to the crowd, and the crowd whistled back to him. He was seventeen, and his mother said he was sleeping so much because he was a growing boy. "It's the age for falling asleep sometimes unexpectedly," she told the reporters. "He's a good boy. Try to be nice to him about it." In the next inning, he hit an inside-the-park home run, and the crowed whistled again, and he laughed and shrugged and waved back to the crowd. He went into the dugout, put on his pads, and took a short nap.

Still, after every game the shortstop waited until everyone had left the stadium, and then he lay down in the grass in the outfield, slowed down his senses, and listened to the low sound coming up from the earth. But since Isabella's coming back to life, it felt strange to the shortstop, lying in the outfield. The shortstop had a pretty good idea of how time worked, that the moments were not continuous, and that any event took up a discrete number of indivisible moments. The shortstop could feel himself moving through time like you can feel yourself moving through water. He was careful to notice how it felt, and he had a pretty good idea that he could feel each individual moment rubbing up against him, especially on his neck. Sometimes, waking up, the feeling snuck up on him and sent a shiver into his ribcage. Lying in the outfield, he often felt he could make out each moment perfectly, and soon he would start to notice the space between one moment and the next, and then he would begin to sense the space between any two moments growing, until any two moments were as far from each other as stars, with a great void between them, into which the shortstop might disappear for as long as he pleased. There was a chance of the shortstop getting agoraphobic in these enormous empty spaces, and once he had felt the air sucked straight out of him, and he'd had to cover his mouth with his hands from the feeling that his lungs might also get sucked out.

But now, since Isabella had woken up, the empty space seemed less empty to the shortstop. The gaps between each moment now seemed occupied by a great prehistoric creaking, like a far-off tsunami wave, some awful, ramshackle thing, some vast presence, held together by luck and misfortune. It made the shortstop feel the gravity loosening around him, and his knees would wobble when he finally got up and left the stadium.

Thirty-five. Harry Names the Stadium

After his first dream of dancing with Valentina Tereshkova, the first woman in space, the ex-president woke up and filled a brandy snifter with cold water and drank it down. Then he did it again. Then he did it three more times. Then he let out a big burp.

In his waking life, he had never loved Valentina Tereshkova very much, and he had never asked anyone to call him Harry. No one had called the ex-president Harry in many years. He'd gotten so he very much liked not being called Harry. Finally, he had said to his wife, "Please don't call me Harry."

"What should I call you then, dear?" she'd asked.

"Call me Mr. Senator, or Captain. I've always deeply enjoyed *Captain*."

That was when Harry's wife started looking at him like he was a stranger, and at that moment Harry began feeling much more comfortable. He felt his jaw untense, just a little bit. He gave his wife a smile and touched her on the shoulder. "In emergencies I suppose you might call me *dear*," he said, smiling even bigger.

Benjamin had persisted in calling Harry Harry until Harry was president. Then Benjamin called Harry Harry one last time, about two hours after the inauguration, giving Harry a hug and saying, "Harry. How do you feel?"

"God damn it, Benjamin," Harry said. "You will call me Mr. President or you will call me nothing at all." Benjamin called his brother nothing at all until he was no longer president. Then Benjamin started to call him Mr. President.

Now the ex-president imagined he might very well enjoy Harry. He had many more dreams asking Valentina to call him Harry. "Please Valentina," he would say. "Please try." Valentina could only blush and look away.

After one dream, Harry called Benjamin and asked if Benjamin might call him Harry. "You're a hopeless old shit," said Benjamin, and hung up the telephone.

Waking from a dream in which Valentina had fallen on the dance floor and badly hurt her elbow, and Harry had threatened to withhold first aid unless she called him Harry, it occurred to Harry that he had not named his baseball stadium. Everyone simply called it "the stadium" or "the Argentinean stadium." Harry had refused all corporate offers to buy the stadium's name, but he had not named it. He considered calling it Harry Park, or Harry Field. He decided on Stadium Harry. At the ceremony he made a speech and insisted that everyone call him Harry, or, if they absolutely must, Mr. Harry.

They started calling the dinosaur laboratory, too, Stadium Harry. Harry decided that the dinosaur too needed a name, and he named her Elizabeth, which actually sounded to Isabella quite like her real name.

Thirty-six. Isabella's New Lifestyle

Isabella could do a lap of her big room at Stadium Harry in about three minutes, at a very leisurely pace. Isabella only ever moved at a leisurely pace around Stadium Harry. Even if Isabella did once in a while get an itch to kick and run, just for the feeling of it, to remind her muscles what they were especially good for, still she never did it. She could read the nervousness in the people who came to leave her food, or take away her dung. Even the people who watched her from the next room through the big bulletproof window seemed ridiculously nervous. Even Penelope, who had taken to bringing a rocking chair with her into the dinosaur room and sitting down and rocking and reading books to Isabella, playing a melody on her flügelhorn every now and then, and who had gone so far as to pat Isabella on the nose, Isabella could tell that even Penelope worried what Isabella might do, and that everyone's general nervousness would not be eased if Isabella took even just a quick romp around the room.

When Penelope read to Isabella, she spoke much too quickly for Isabella to follow. Dinosaur speech is slow and methodical, to accommodate their thick, lumbering tongues and their heavy memories. Each generation of dinosaur spoke more slowly than the last, and spoke less, as if there was simply too much already on everyone's mind to bother speaking, or perhaps they had simply come to such a perfect understanding of each other that there was little left to say, until their mouths were just agile enough to eat, and they spoke as clumsily as they ate. Penelope's speech, by comparison, flickered like a hummingbird.

But in Isabella's last life, she had been able to understand hummingbirds. Hummingbirds communicated in a kind of rapid Morse code with their wingbeats, and punctuated and inflected their wingbeats with successions of barely audible squeaks. Isabella had always admired their language for its perfect timing. Hummingbirds had an uncanny humor based entirely on timing, and when Isabella was entirely exhausted after a trying swim, she liked nothing better than to listen to a hummingbird, or two hummingbirds joking together. Isabella had understood the language of just about everything, the austere language of bees, the mourning language of frogs, and so on. Of course there were exceptions, a jubilant frog, or a sober dolphin, but generally a thing's condition was shaped by the tone of its language. There was the wind, stringing together an endless series of aphorisms in its wind-speak. There was the water, with its many dialectical tongues. Her speech was as slow as any dinosaur's, but Isabella's hearing had been quick, and she had been able to hear and follow all the rapid languages around her.

Now she couldn't follow Penelope's. Perhaps she had lost something of herself to the ice.

Then she started to notice something in Penelope's speech. Penelope was calling Isabella by name. "Why, Elizabeth, you're looking fine today," Penelope might say. Or, "What do you think of that, Elizabeth?" It was close enough that Isabella guessed that this must be what her name sounded like in Penelope's language, that it was as close as Penelope could come to pronouncing "Isabella."

With this one glimpse of recognition, it was a simple thing for Isabella to sort out the gist of Penelope's language. It was a less simple thing to sort out the fine points of the grammar, but after a few months, Isabella had managed it. She experimented, sneaking human words in among the dinosaur words she often spoke to herself for practice, which the scientists of course took for senseless groaning.

Thirty-seven. Iple Examines a Fish

It's easy enough to look in on life on Earth from the afterlife. People like to watch over their loved ones and their loved things. Especially their loved things. The first stranger Iple had demonstrated his knife trick for, this stranger only looked to Earth to keep watch over a certain fountain pen with which he had written a series of letters that had gradually broken his heart. He told Iple, "Once the pen is gone—and it has been treated with particular carelessness by its most recent owner—there will be nothing left on Earth for me."

"Well, let me show you something," said Iple, and he showed the butterfly trick to the stranger.

There were rules for looking at Earth. There were designated public looking areas, so that what you looked at could be noticed. The dead were treated with suspicion always, but especially when looking in on Earth. A close watch was kept on them. Perhaps by no one but one another. Performing his knife trick so many times, Iple began to understand that the dead policed themselves fastidiously. Watching their loved ones and their loved things was a vice, but it was forgivable, as long as a close watch was kept. Iple guessed that there must be a very wrong way to look back at Earth, some unspoken prohibition, and so he soon kept away from the public looking areas.

Iple wondered if he might also die out of the afterlife. If in his life they had been playing a joke on him, this now seemed a more awful joke. He considered it and wandered, no one visible in any direction, and experimented, since the world still yielded some considerable surprises. He had learned that he could whittle his fingertip all day with his knife, until his finger was so sharp that he could spear a fish with it, and that if he closed his eyes and wished for his fingertip back, it was back.

So when he saw his first fish, he took out his knife and quickly whittled his finger into a spear, stuck the fish, and held it up to give it a look. He held it by its spine like he was holding the spine of a book. The fish wiggled its head back and forth and back and forth, and then it wiggled its tail back and forth and back and forth, as if it were running tests on itself, trying to figure out why it wasn't swimming anymore. Iple took out his knife and slit open the fish's whole belly and spread it open with his fingers.

Iple wasn't surprised. Inside the fish he could see anything he wanted of life on Earth. He wasn't sure he wanted to see any of it. He remembered how the colors had always been too intense, the smells too intense, the sounds, when he could hear them, had been too intense, and when he could not hear them, the silences too were too intense. He felt nauseated at the memory of it, and his legs fell out from under him as perfectly as if he had meant them to. From the sitting position, he thought he might look in on Penelope and her flügelhorn, and there she was, sitting in her rocking chair, playing her flügelhorn for Isabella, exactly as Iple had imagined it might sound.

Iple patched up the fish's belly with some wet ginkgo leaves and let it back into the water, and it swam out past where Iple could see beneath the water's surface.

Thirty-eight. Reincarnation

No person comes back from the afterlife to life on Earth. Iple got in the habit of staring back at life on Earth for whole days at a time, watching Penelope lie on her sofa and listen to the radio, a wet washcloth over her face, or watching Isabella work a pile of vegetation around in her maw.

Iple would hide himself away and then open his fish like an encyclopedia and hypnotize himself in it, and get washed in a numinous intoxication. Iple had the idea more than once to try to crawl through the fish back into the world. He reached his arm into its belly, or his foot, or he tried to pull it down over his head like a winter hat. Each time, the fish would go to pieces, and it would take Iple some hours to paste the whole thing back together and set it back into the water. The fish had grown fond of Iple, and swam to him when they noticed he was near. But they were only little mirrors with which Iple might peek around an untraversable corner back at life.

Still, watching Earth, Iple noticed certain suggestive resonances. He saw his fourth grade teacher perfectly incarnate in a girl teaching herself to whistle while she wandered deep into the tall, silvery pampas grass. Iple's fourth grade teacher died almost the same way Iple did. She had a sleepwalker husband, and sleepwalking he attacked her in her sleep with bits of glass from a smashed carafe.

Now here she was, a totally new girl, Iple was sure it was her. Even if she couldn't remember how to whistle. And how had she made it back incarnate and not him, Iple wanted to know.

It is something that no one has any memory of. When a thing dies, it's rent. Some is rent into the afterlife, and some stays right where it is and decays with the body, and some is rent back into ordinary life, utterly amnesic. The population in the afterlife keeps growing, but the population in the world does not; it is the same worn-out souls circulating and recirculating, picking up memories and then dropping them when they die, then picking up more and dropping them again. You have to look back to the very first pinprick of time to find such a thing as a young consciousness.

Iple can almost guess this, but not quite. He's been reincarnated as a train station in the Midwestern United States, but he will never recognize himself in it.

Thirty-nine. Zebedee's Figurehead

After Zebedee drove into the gas station, Esther the pizza store owner took care of Zebedee's things. Zebedee left a will, and the will said for Esther to do what she would with his things, which, said his will, were few. He had two suitcases' worth of things, including two suitcases. The suitcases were in his hotel room. One held clothes, which he had put away in the hotel's closet and dresser. The clothes were fine, and the right size for Esther's boy Gottlieb, so she packed them into their suitcase to take to Gottlieb.

The other suitcase held five dictionaries. A Russian, a Spanish, a Mandarin, an Urdu, and a Swahili. It held a slide whistle and a thumb piano, a small box of photographs, and the baby quilt Zebedee's mother's mother had sewn for him. Esther kept this suitcase zipped-up in a corner of her attic.

Zebedee put nothing in his will about his house where he kept the figurehead, or about the figurehead itself. Zebedee had made arrangements to leave the house untouched, so that the figurehead sat there quiet and untouched, not even gathering any dust, really, not even any light getting on it, but for a dim, soft filtration through the heavy curtains.

In the afterlife, Zebedee had trouble keeping his hands and feet warm. He understood it as some penance for the gambling luck he'd enjoyed in his life on Earth, which it was, though from what he could tell, no one had sentenced him to any penance, nor seen to it. Zebedee'd had no particular love for the luck he'd had gambling, and now he paid no particular mind to his cold hands and feet. Some times he'd rub his feet together, or his hands, or rub his feet with his hands, or hold his hands in his armpits, or fold his feet into his knee pits, to

PAUL FATTARUSO

try to warm them up, but most of the time he just forgot and let them go cold.

He came to the public viewing area about once a month, to have a look at the figurehead. He'd met Charlotte there in the afterlife, touched her face, kissed her cheekbones. Watching her perform her old gestures again, he was scared, they were so easy for her. The way she held onto his arm, or touched at the ends of his mustache.

Soon, though, Zebedee preferred to visit the figurehead, which seemed somehow to remind him more of Charlotte than Charlotte herself did. Zebedee doubted whether the Charlotte of the afterlife was Charlotte at all, as convincingly Charlotte as she was. He suspected that the real Charlotte had been incarnated into the figurehead. Which she had. So had Zebedee. A disproportionate number of people chose life as that figurehead for their next life on Earth. It was a regular sinkhole for reincarnations. Zebedee could almost recognize himself in it. He doubted, as convincing as it seemed to be, whether this afterlife was anything real, whether this was him, or if he wasn't just stranded on Earth and dead.

Meanwhile, the figurehead sat in its quiet little house, filling up with quiet old unmemoried souls.

Forty. The Flügelhorn

Playing the flügelhorn passably is not such a difficult thing to do. It's not so different from a trumpet or a cornet. Any trumpeter or cornetist might pick up a flügelhorn and get a decent sound out of it. But there is a subtler tone in the flügelhorn, and this tone waits in the horn and sounds out only when someone who knows exactly how to blow through it blows through it. Then the flügelhorn gives up its secret. Every thing has a secret it doesn't give up easily. Learning one thing's secret, you can almost begin to imagine that you've learned the secret of all things. That is how Penelope played the flügelhorn.

She could do it because the flügelhorn had a voice that was nearly Penelope's own natural voice. She had a kind of understanding with it that way, and an empathy for it, and the flügelhorn seemed to have an empathy for her too. Penelope found this mastery of the flügelhorn when she was twelve, and it had brought Benjamin to tears every night for two months, alternately with admiration and envy, he who had only ever tinkled pitifully on the piano and would die without finding the secret of any musical thing.

Isabella recognized the language of Penelope's flügelhorn immediately as one of the irreducible languages, and it put her at ease to hear it. It resolved her to trust Penelope. Isabella continued to practice her English on the sly, anticipating at what moment she might speak to Penelope. When she grew too tired to enunciate, Isabella retreated back into her memories to reckon what she might say.

Forty-one. Isabella's Swim to Antarctica

It was a rainy springtime, and Isabella was moving with a pack of dinosaurs through Egypt. At sunset, the sky turned color and hunched in closer to the Earth. Then the color left it entirely, and it lost its taste. Isabella picked a few wild carrots out of the sand for dinner. Her head wavered with the after-image of mirage-ripples, and blood fluttered in her eyelids. An evening rain came on and cast a faint rainbow around the moon. All the dinosaurs went to sleep in one fell moment.

Isabella woke up with her face wet from tears, barely able to draw air, her chest compacting. The moon had moved maybe two minutes' worth in its arc.

It wasn't so unusual for a dinosaur to up and leave a pack in the night. The pack wakes up to find one missing, and the pack will perhaps linger a little over its breakfast. Then they leave. The disappeared dinosaur might return to the pack in a week, sometimes many years later, sometimes not ever. Isabella couldn't remember what she'd dreamt, but she knew it meant for her to leave. She padded off toward the Red Sea. A cadre of iridescent-backed insects went with her, sometimes getting off ahead into the horizon, then coming back to her. When she'd gotten far enough away from her sleeping pack, she threw into a full gallop. She reached the coast as the moon set, and launched her dark, silent body into the water.

She let it wash her away from the coast. Isabella knew a sin-gular thing about moving through the water. She could choose to be carried or not carried by any wave. She could catch her foot on even the most muted current and dance it to its outer edge through any mighty countercurrent. She could climb the giant wave's back and look out to the horizons from its upper lip, her legs working methodically through its crazed water, or she might nuzzle the giant wave teasingly in its curl, or she might swim straight through it as she would swim in still lake water. The night she set swim for Antarctica, the Red Sea was just lapping mildly to shore, and she glided herself out into it almost unconsciously. Through the night, thin fogs rose up out of the sea, bending pale fragments of color out of the moon-light, and then fell back into the sea.

Isabella spent most of her swim in a sort of dream. It was part of why she loved swimming, that her thoughts had the tendency to sink. From her head, they flushed down into her body, an intelligence of motion, her legs tracing their series of ellipses, her tail, propellering. Then, once the swim-move-ments became reflexive, her thoughts would dislodge from her body entirely and drift down into the water. At first, she could see her heavy silhouette, churning at the surface, and the light from the sun, chopped up by the flux of the sea-top. But as her thoughts sank deeper, she couldn't make out her figure, and the sun diminished. Isabella considered the sun not so much obscured as peeled down to its meager insides. She imagined that it must taste like a mouthful of ginger root. Then the sun would disappear entirely, and Isabella's thoughts, when they sank like this, were no longer hers to have. They worked on their own, and left her to make her way around automatically. By the time she dried off, they had invariably made their way back into her head, fatigued and freshened.

She navigated the Red Sea like this, towing her thoughts across the seabed, or her thoughts towing her, through the Gulf of Aden, skirting the Arabian Sea and into the Indian Ocean, down through the Mozambique Channel, she went along in a dream, and the dream kept secret from her, scratching its way along the floor of the ocean.

Isabella lurched back awake still four days' swim from Antarctica, starving, her joints stiffening. She dove and caught herself a fish. She had never eaten a fish. Its gnashed bone parti-cles scraped on the soft tissue in her long throat. The water was so cold it pulled the air out of her. Her breath came in quick, great bursts of steam, with loud involuntary bellows. Isabella kept swimming south, into the cold, and the gradual slowing down, convinced that she had set a destination for herself.

She dove often, to find fish and to keep the water from freezing to her face, and tried to shake out of her consciousness, to make the time pass, but it would not go.

She taught herself a new, minimal, loping stroke, in which she mimicked the lope of the water itself. It was almost as effortless as holding still. Her body stung like nothing in her memory, and she fought to hold down mouthfuls of air. When she saw the enormous stretch of ice on the horizon, she knew this was what her thoughts had been thinking of without her.

Forty-two. The Far-Distant Past

It's helpful to know that in the far-distant past, even before the dinosaurs, there were people, ordinary human beings, just like now, only slightly smaller, and they lived longer. On average, they lived to be one hundred fourteen years old, according to their own calculations. They made calculations often, and they made their calculations carefully. They made beautifully calculated buildings in beautifully calculated locations. Even before they had calculators, even before they had an abacus, the people of the far-distant past had a knack and a passion for calculating. Their farms, their hats, their rowboats, the oars of their rowboats, their shoes and shoelaces, and their wheelbarrows were all painstakingly calculated. Their mills and their trains were calculated. Their television programs were calculated, their schedules, their indiscretions, their vices, their fears and their loves, which were of course affected by the calculations themselves, in which case the calculations had to be included in the calculations—a complex but not impossible process. Their roads and their smokestacks and their booby traps, their soapdishes and their skyscrapers, their barbecues were calculated and their baseball games were extensively calculated. They had baseball, almost the same as baseball today. They had the infield fly rule, and the ground-rule double rule, and the balk rule. They had the batter's box, though it was slightly smaller. The bat and the ball and the field were all slightly smaller, and the bases and the dugout were slightly smaller. Just slightly. Less than an inch.

They had inches. Later, they had centimeters. They even had furlongs. They had petticoats, zeppelins, butterfly nets, cameras, guitars, urinals, and potholders. They had fountain pens, and then they had click-pens. They had hysterectomies and revolutions and dog breeders. They had lace and cheese and power-saws and crossword puzzles. They had airports and in the airports they had moving walkways. They had just about everything. Two things they did not have were ginger ale and eggplant parmesan.

But one thing they definitely did have was a penchant for calculating. When they ran out of other things to calculate, they calculated probabilities. They made great advances in weather and baseball. The statisticians of the far-distant past began successfully predicting thundershowers and triple plays months in advance. No more rainy-day weddings, and people went to the baseball games to cheer the eerie fulfillments of predictions.

Then a little girl, with no calculator at all, and none of the necessary contextual data, correctly predicted the exact times of seventeen consecutive lightning strikes on the other side of the planet. Soon after, she predicted the delivery of a truckload of expired milk to her elementary school, the pregnancy of her second grade teacher, her mother's sprained ankle on the tread-mill, and the mysterious arrival of fourteen kittens on the doorstep of her next-door neighbor.

Then one morning the little girl's father was reading a golf magazine and eating his breakfast of oat cereal and strawber-ries, and his little girl shouted from the other room, "Stop right there, daddy. Do *not* eat that strawberry." She said it just like a girl-voiced army general. Her daddy looked at the strawberry on his spoon, and standing there on his strawberry was a furry, cherry-sized spider. He dropped the spoon and the strawberry and the spider back into his cereal bowl and covered the bowl over with plastic wrap and started on a loud, convulsive fit of crying. The little girl's daddy, like almost everyone of the far-distant past, had gone slowly and quietly unnerved at the thought of living in an utterly predictable world, as the politi-cians were promising we all would within the decade. The daddy had gone so much unnerved that he'd started waking up with the taste of vomit in the back of his throat, and his breathing stuttered when he found himself in large crowds. They were common symptoms for the average person living at that particularly momentous time in the far-distant past.

Forty-three. Eliza

The little girl sat down and cried at the breakfast table with her daddy. She cried in a low, steady sob. The way she cried, she sounded like she might fall asleep any second, though in fact it was breakfast time and she had just woken up and she was feeling wide awake and quite perky. She teared profusely. The tears wet her cheeks and dribbled down around the corners of her mouth. They dripped down to her chin and down her neck, wetting her shirt collar. Thin, teary snot rolled out her nose, and more than once she blew a bubble of it.

Her daddy cried more violently, a sharp, spastic fit, with periodic strange belches. He made almost no tears, and a few times the little girl wet her hands on her cheeks and rubbed the tears onto her daddy, smearing them mostly into his eyebrows and mustache. She went on like crying this, beside her daddy, until she guessed that he might be sensible enough to answer a question. Then she asked him, in a kind of sobby moan, "Why do you think you're crying, daddy?"

At that, her daddy cried harder than ever, and at one point buckled over in a terrible, prolonged belch. So she went ahead crying herself. When he seemed almost able to catch his breath, she asked him again, "So daddy, what are you crying about? Are you afraid of spiders? Did something bad happen with a spider once?" She wiped her nose on the shoulder of her shirt, watching closely for his answer.

"Oh," he said, and then a last, mild burp. "It's not the spider so much. It's just that, between you and those statisticians, I imagine that if you wanted to, you could predict my entire life. Which makes my actual living seem, just, superfluous."

She looked at him amazed. "Superfluous?"

"You know, extra and unnecessary."

She stood up on her chair and said to him, frowning and serious, "That is a very odd idea."

Her mother named her Elizabeth, after a character from a romance film. When she was old enough to talk, she said, "Don't call me Elizabeth. Call me *Eliza*."

Forty-four. Eliza and the Statistician

The reporters were the first ones to dote on Eliza. Over the three days after her lightning bolt predictions, she appeared on thirty-two evening news programs. The reporters all gave her lollipops. Over the aforementioned three-day period, she accumulated seventy-one lollipops, including one sassafras, one sarsaparilla, and one horehound. Eliza stored her lollipops in her humble collection of music boxes.

After the reporters came the statisticians. One statistician representative came to visit Eliza. His fellow statisticians considered him an especially likable statistician, and they often called on him in situations that required finesse, charm, and discretion. When an unfortunate prediction had revealed itself in the statistics, like a volcano due to smother a tiny tropical paradise, or a star pitcher about to permanently lose control of his fastball, the statisticians all looked to this one particular statistician to negotiate the terms of the prediction with the public, and the public accepted this statistician's bad news and admired him for being the one to tell it to them, and they understood that it was not a job he enjoyed and that he did it because it was what was to be done and he would do it and he was not sentimental about it, and yet he was never without the proper aspect of regret for bad news. It was something he was good at.

He was good at it because he loved statistics. He loved them though sometimes they rained an unpleasant fire down on the human beings, as when the statisticians learned that the Earth was due for a bombardment of tiny meteor particles, most of which would burn up in the atmosphere, but some of which would make it through, tiny, smoldering, furious bits of space rock, and that they would burn holes in our rooftops and set fire to forests, that corn and cows would be lost, that possibly some whole villages would be lost, though unfortunately the statisticians could not be entirely sure which villages, and so forth. He loved even these statistics, because they were awful, yes, but they were just coincidentally awful. They were just awful because they were telling the truth, which he could not believe was a bad thing to do, and in this way, with the statistics themselves as his model, the statistician found a way to share the awful statistical messages with his fellow ladies and gentlemen.

He brought Eliza a bag of chocolate coins and they sat down on the couch together. "I imagine you've been very busy these past few days, Eliza," said the statistician. Eliza nodded.

"Well let me ask you an old question," he said. "How do you think you predicted those lightning-strikes?" He was a very brave statistician.

"I was just thinking about lightning, and wondering when it might lightning. Then, all of a sudden, I thought I had a very good idea of when it might lightning. So I wrote down the times."

"So I've heard," said the statistician. Eliza enjoyed the statistician's bravery, and wanted to pay him a compliment, but he looked as if he were about to go on saying something. Then he went on. "Well, it's very interesting. People have been known to make some unusually accurate and extraordinary predictions, but yours, I'm afraid, are exasperatingly extraordinary.

"You're probably aware that we're working on our own science of prediction, my fellow statisticians and I. And we're proud of the progress we've made. You're too young to remember this, but there was a time when nothing could be decently predicted even a day ahead of time. *Yes.*"

The statistician paused, as if contemplating the dark, unpredictable past.

"We have come a long way," he went on. "Of course, we monitor an enormous amount of activity, and record it, and process it, and cross-tabulate, and so on, really quite massive amounts of data, and, naturally, more massive amounts each passing minute. It becomes quite a task just isolating an event to predict, actually. But we do it, and we do it, if I may say so, fairly well. I think we have spared more heartache than we have caused. And there are very few organizations that can make a claim like that. But you." Here the statistician paused and waved a finger at Eliza, almost flirtatiously.

"You have managed to predict things that we could not have predicted, and without the help of even one abnormally large calculator, of which we, naturally, have countless. That, to my knowledge, is a unique accomplishment." Now the statistician gestured to Eliza whether she might give him one of her chocolate coins. She tore the bag open with her teeth and handed him a coin in the largest of three sizes. The statistician pulled apart the foil and popped the coin into his mouth.

Then he went on, his mouth working a little slowly, "Well, we think you might be able to help us. We think you might be able to do a great deal of good. Saving lives and so forth."

Eliza looked like she was ready to sneeze. It was her "poker face." Her dad had taught her to practice a poker face for times when she didn't want people to know what she was thinking, and so far, this was the best she could come up with. Her dad said it was good enough, that he certainly couldn't tell what she was thinking when she made that face. It made the statistician uneasy. "Do you have to sneeze?" he asked. She shook her head no and held her poker face, and eventually he took a cellular phone from the inside pocket of his sports coat and handed it to her.

"I want you to have this," he said. "If you have any more predictions, just turn it on, and someone will be there to listen. Or, if you just want to say hello, or you have any questions … Oh, here's a stray hair." The statistician picked a stray hair off Eliza's shoulder and put it in his pocket. Eliza turned on her new phone, and it picked up immediately.

"Yes," came a strange statistician's voice.

"I think your grandmother gave you a little accordion, and you keep it on your dresser," said Eliza.

"That's very good," said the strange statistician's voice. "It's called a *concertina*."

Forty-five. Eliza and Her Duplicate

Eliza tried but could not understand her father's fear of accurate predictions. The first third of every evening news broadcast was dedicated to a rundown of the day's fulfilled predictions, and now Eliza noticed how her father turned a minty, sick green during this part of the news broadcast. She understood that when his expression glazed over, as it often did, it meant he'd slipped into his state of fatalistic vertigo. Then she would go to the silverware drawer and throw spoons at him as hard as she could until he stopped it.

At times, Eliza wondered if her father might be playing an elaborate joke on her, his angst seemed so pitifully senseless. At last she said to him, "You know, dad, I think it would be far more frightening to live in an unpredictable world. How would you know that there was a future there at all, waiting for you, without the predictions? How can you be sure you won't live right off the edge of time, and fall into something really awful? It's just like seeing. How could you even know you had hands, really, if you couldn't see them? Seeing is good. And helpful. You shouldn't be afraid of it. It's just a part of life. It makes absolutely no sense to be so afraid of it. Try to be a little brave."

Eliza's father rushed to the sink and vomited all over the dirty dishes. Eliza knew it was hopeless. She turned on her cellular phone.

"Yes?" answered the concertina statistician.

"I'm afraid I won't be making any more predictions," said Eliza.

"Oh, girl. Come on now," said the concertina statistician, which was what he often said to his own daughter, who was just about Eliza's age.

"No, that's it," said Eliza.

The concertina statistician sighed. "Well, that's a downright shame. But not entirely unexpected."

"OK," said Eliza, and she turned off her cellular phone and buried it in some damp coffee grounds in the kitchen trash.

But the statisticians were already working on another Eliza, using genetic material from the stray hair stolen off Eliza's shoulder during her meeting with the statistician. An outstanding lady statistician was chosen to be surrogate mother to the duplicate Eliza. It was an easy pregnancy, and an uncomplicated cesarean section, and they pulled the mucus from the duplicate baby's throat, and the baby coughed and coughed but it did not cry, and the statisticians all gathered together for a picture with the baby and its mother, and they named it Elizabeth, just like the original, but for short they called her Beth.

They gave Beth a good variety of fruits and vegetables, and taught her the names of things. The concertina statistician taught her how to play the concertina. They took her on trips into town, and they took her on trips to the country. Her surrogate mother taught her reading, and then history, and then literature. She taught her a little math, but not too much. All the statisticians were very careful not to give Beth too many statistics too soon. They didn't talk about their work around her. When predictions came up by chance in a conversation, they all made a point to feign indifference, although not too suspiciously much indifference.

Forty-six. Beth's Coming-of-Age

bib [ical (handwritten marginal note)

The statisticians were patient, and the time came when Beth started sprouting predictions, as effortlessly as pubes. With a mouthful of waffle, she declared that a small velvety black-skinned frog would momentarily emerge from her shower drain, and anyone intending to handle the frog must wear rubber gloves and goggles, because the frog likes to spit a blinding venom from a gland on its back.

They celebrated this first prediction with strawberry shortcake at lunchtime and tuna casserole at dinner. Two of Beth's favorites. She stuffed herself and went to bed with a clear, happy head. She woke up with twenty-three predictions, and had fifty-two more during the day. That night they had a party with cake and candles, and Beth's surrogate mother put her hands on Beth's cheeks and said she always knew Beth was an extraordinary little girl, and kissed her forehead. The statisticians were joyous. They praised her until bedtime. The next morning, she awoke with ninety-eight predictions, saving twelve lives and a large condominium complex. Why, the statisticians now wondered, had they made only one of her?

None of the catastrophes she predicted seemed to unsettle her. "A speckled foal will land badly from a long fall down an elevator shaft," she might say flatly. Then she gave the date and time and location and went on with whatever thing she was up to, lunch or a ballet lesson or a game of Go. The concertina statistician had spent considerable time teaching her Go, in hopes that it might help her predicting, that it might remind her to consider the effects of her previous predictions when formulating a new one. He invented cause-and-effect exercises for her, though Beth told him more than once that he was superstitious to worry so much about causes and effects.

Beth's surrogate mother worried that some of the more awful predictions might traumatize Beth, and tried to have a talk with her at bedtime. "Some of these things, they're truly awful, darling. They give me nightmares. That girl with the broken bottle today, she was born the week after you were. It's natural to be afraid, or shocked. I'm shocked, and I've been around much longer than you have. It's alright if you're shocked."

Beth sat up into a half-lotus position in her pajamas. "I know," she said. "But I don't feel very shocked. The things just occur to me. Like facts. I don't have any choice about it, but they don't have any choice about it either. A lot of the time, I think, events are embarrassed that I'm noticing them. I think events are very shy things. I feel embarrassed for them. But I think it makes it easier if I don't act embarrassed. So I try to act natural. But that's not the same as shocked." Beth looked thoughtful, and then she nodded. "I'm pretty sure I'm alright. And I don't think you'll have nightmares for much longer. And get this cuspid looked at tomorrow," she said, pointing to her surrogate mother's cuspid.

Beth went to sleep speculating that her body might be full of miniature, empty staircases, and nothing else.

↳ "good exercise," but also surprise at the bottom

Forty-seven. Beth's Trip to the City

After a month of miraculous predicting, Beth received an invitation to the capitol city, to a dinner in her honor, at which world leaders and great authors and tycoons' wives might get a chance to set their own eyes on her and ask her a few carefully worded questions. Beth had never visited a major city, though she had seen many movies.

The statisticians went and bought her a new dress and a ribbon for her hair, and instructed her in the proper use of various forks. The concertina statistician bought her a pair of binoculars, to use from the tops of tall buildings.

She rode there in the way-back seat of her surrogate mother's minivan, mesmerizing herself in the blur of the highway shoulder. The outer ring of the capitol city was just about to send hints of itself up over the horizon, the faint gaseous plumes of the tallest smokestacks were wisping into view, when Beth spotted a great black blur of a thing lying near the road, on a patch of grassy incline. It went by too fast to tell what it was. Beth undid her seatbelt and turned in her seat to use her binoculars on it through the back window. It was a grown bear with a plastic grocery bag wrapped over its head, suffocated and drawing clouds of flies.

The sight of it triggered a prediction so sudden it made her laugh. Then she covered her mouth to stop herself. She wanted to take that first laugh back. She went cold with a deep, delirious embarrassment.

Forty-eight. Penelope and the Genes

Penelope kept her laboratory in a shed next to a row of greenhouses. For a few hours each afternoon, the sky reflected darkly and exactly in the greenhouse glass, and Penelope tended to lose her laboratorial concentration, staring away into the glass, watching the multiple parallel flights of one bird at various angles of reflection among the many panes, and occasionally the passing of a singular bird-shadow.

Penelope put Isabella's genes through every sort of microscope. She gave them chemical baths, shuffled them and unshuffled them, nudged them, mocked them, scolded them, and generally worshiped them. She checked them against elephant genes and whale genes, and giraffe and kangaroo genes. She visited Isabella every evening with storybooks and her flügelhorn, each time casing Isabella for some vital clue, some thread to lead her beyond the vast obviousness of the dinosaur. But Penelope could make out only the absolute visible wonder of her, how Isabella seemed carved and polished out of flawless, ancient mahogany, and her nails, like gingerly stones, her velvety inner-workings.

It occurred to Penelope one afternoon, staring off at the greenhouses, that she was further from solving the fundamental mystery than she had ever been. The mystery of the dinosaur and its unnaturally large genetic materials, though formidable and compelling, was entirely secondary to that central riddle she had hoped to solve, of which Isabella was only one of endless possible variations. Fussing over the Isabella question, Penelope now understood, she steadily lost the real imperative of her life's research. A helicopter's shadow swooped over the greenhouses. *Shadows*, thought Penelope. *Shadows are a good lead. Shadows will lead me straight to the fundamental mystery. My own shadow will be a loyal informant. I could get back on the case this moment.*

Penelope was already in tears. She would not investigate shadows. She would go on with the irresistible investigation of Isabella, and table her old work indefinitely. Weeping took her over. She took out her flügelhorn, though she could hardly hold her embouchure through her melancholy. She played so perfectly the birds stopped flying to listen.

Forty-nine. Iple's Messages

Iple hid out. His hair and his beard grew, and his skin shrunk tight to his ribs. His orange eyes sunk, and an obsessed look sunk into them. He stopped eating entirely. Eating was a formality in the afterlife, but it was a formality everyone respected. The afterlife, it turned out, was nothing more than a slew of well-guarded formalities and prohibitions, from which Iple duly retreated, to stare into fish-bellies at life on Earth, which went on more or less as he remembered it, though now he noticed he loved it more.

He watched a lot of Penelope. He watched her until he couldn't remember what she looked like. Even as he watched her, he couldn't guess what she looked like. He watched her until he saw her memories, until the actual world around her dissolved and the slightly miscolored space of her memory took over. He watched her memories of things she herself didn't know she remembered. He watched her until the space of her memory faded away, revealing an opulent landscape of fears and desires, by which he was transfixed. He watched until his trusty inner clock stopped, and he took no notice of it, and went on being transfixed. His hair stopped growing. His skin stopped renewing. The obsessed look fell out of his eyes.

Then Penelope played her perfect, bird-stopping song on the flügelhorn. Her song of farewell to her long hope of solving the fundamental mystery, and through the dirge of it burst hints at her million conciliatory joys. Iple awoke from his transfixion already in tears, and he wept as he watched Penelope work the valves on her flügelhorn, and he kept weeping until she finished, and his weeping trailed off, and he slept, which was a formality in the afterlife, but he did it.

He woke and ate and trimmed his hair and beard nice and neat. He whipped the wrinkles out of his tie and tied it with a deft, expert Windsor maneuver. He fashioned himself a fishing rod, and fished a fine desk and chair from the creek. He left them in the sun to dry while he manicured himself and cleaned his teeth. He sat down at the desk to write to Penelope. He reached down and picked a blade of grass. He took a fine, fine chisel from the desk drawer. He wanted to write, *Dearest Penelope, I have solved the fundamental mystery and want to assure you that it is a serious disappointment, like all solutions. Take heart. You've hedged against a much deeper regret than your current one. I remain as devoted and helpless as ever. Iple.*

Iple knew that if he wrote it, he would catch someone's unwanted attention, that a wrath would come looking for him. Plus the blade of grass was too small. So he limited himself. "A lucky detective is the one with many pending mysteries," he chiseled into the grass, and he fed the grass to the fish, and let the fish into the creek to find its way to Penelope. He chiseled into a hundred more blades and fed them to a hundred more fish. Then he ate, and then chiseled a thousand more blades of grass. Then he chiseled one hundred thousand, and fed them to one hundred thousand fish. His hands and eyes did not ache. At some point, his trusty inner clock resumed.

Fifty. Isabella Speaks

Isabella had practiced her English enough. This time, when Penelope entered the dinosaur room, Isabella said, "Hello, Penelope. How is everything," forming the words slowly with her great mouth parts, articulating meticulously.

Penelope showed no sign of surprise. The giant tape-recording machine was as usual spinning away in the devices room. "Oh," said Penelope, "I had an awful melancholy yesterday. I thought I might be done for. But here I am. I think sleeping really helped."

"Good for that," said Isabella. She spoke with a vaguely Swedish accent. After a pause, she said, "You are studying my genetic material, but it's rather stupefying, isn't it. It is monstrously large. Because it is not the product of the usual natural selection." Isabella took a long pause between each sentence, summoning her breath. "Dinosaurs, such as myself, were theorized and engineered by human scientists." Penelope kept quiet. "Not unlike the scientists here, but just a little bit smaller," said Isabella. "Yes," said Isabella. "They had a fully industrialized and technologized society," she said. "Just as ambitious and torrential as this one. Those humans tended to be a tad smaller, as I said. But they wore the same sorts of clothing. And they had the same feverous expression on their faces. They were proud and delirious. A little adolescent girl came along with a gift for prophesying. After one trip to the capitol city, she said that these human beings had no future. That they had very little time left. Other people had given similar warnings, but they took the little adolescent girl seriously. Because she was always frighteningly accurate with her predictions. Every day, she made a few thousand of them. The ones that could be proven were always proven. So they searched the girl for a solution. They proposed massive environmental reforms, disarmament plans, legislated birth control, so on. But the prophet girl said no, it's too late. So they started making strange proposals. Someone proposed genetic engineering, and the prophet girl said perhaps. They called it a 'controlled mutation.' Dinosaurs were the immediate descendants of those human beings. Any dinosaur could tell you who were her, or his, human ancestors. The dinosaurs of my generation still had an atavistic fragment of human consciousness in us. Oh," said Isabella, "what an exhausting language."

Penelope sat there. Isabella rested. Penelope took out a stick of gum and chewed it. She looked at her gum wrapper. "So what happened to all their artifacts? Why haven't archaeologists discovered any evidence of this ancient advanced human civilization? Why haven't we found a city?"

"The girl insisted that it must all go. Every manmade accouterment must disappear. She was firm about it, but never cruel. Still, it broke a lot of people's hearts. They concocted a terrifically elaborate plan to launch everything into space. It was a thirty-year plan. Anything that couldn't be composted would go up in a rocket. Before the rocket plan really took hold, though, a researcher announced his little nanomachines. They were made of forty atoms apiece, and when you let one loose, it would spend the whole day disassembling molecules. At the end of the day, they disassembled themselves. He called them fairies. One fairy could disassemble a whole piano. Seven could do a truck. He taught them how to recognize living tissue, so they wouldn't disassemble anyone's fingertips or gladiolas or so forth. He developed little fairy-kits, and people made the fairies right in their kitchens, and in an hour, the kit and the kitchen were gone. That's why they designed us the way they did. To survive without kitchens and other human accouterments. To survive comfortably. Dinosaurs were only ever seriously hunted by each other. The whole Earth was our kitchen. That was no accident. It was very carefully planned." Penelope spit her gum into its foil paper.

"They had an especially hard time sending the fairies into their libraries," said Isabella. "As I said, it broke a lot of people's hearts. Some of them wondered if they were perhaps improperly trying to negotiate the terms of their own extinction, that it was better to die off and leave a handful of moldy, glorious libraries than to survive as unrecognizable beasts. But this is why my genetic material is as large as it is. Because they learned how to store memories in it. So that once the libraries were gone, and even once the humans were gone, their memories could perpetuate themselves in the dinosaurs. And it worked beautifully. I can access any memory from among the last generation of my human ancestors, and over the generations, my line has accumulated thousands of human ancestors. I can see the old capitol city clearly. I can even remember the moment the little adolescent prophet girl first intuited the humans' extinction, since she herself is among my human ancestors. Along the direct maternal line, as a matter of fact. My mother's mother's mother's so on."

Isabella got a far-away look in her eyes. "Now I think I'd like to take a nap."

"OK, Elizabeth," said Penelope, and Penelope also took a nap.

Fifty-one. The Shortstop's Last Game

It was an early afternoon game against a team of Brazilian firemen who'd had their bats blessed by a monk in Rio de Janeiro. They swung with their eyes closed. The ball came off their bats too fast to even see it. They hit three past the shortstop in the first inning. There would be the crack of the blessed bat, and then the ball skittering around in the outfield, leaving gashes in the turf. All the shortstop could hear was the ball crashing past him. No one knew what to think. The firemen scored eleven runs in the top of the first inning.

The shortstop chewed a stick of gum in the dugout. In the bottom of the first, he hit a triple into the leftfield corner, and stole home on a wild pitch. The shortstop looked at the Brazilians' bats, like radiant tropical birds. He stretched his ankles to get ready to go back into the field. Eleven to one going into the second inning.

The shortstop watched the ball rest in his pitcher's hand, watched his pitcher's fingers find the ball's seams. He lingered in each moment. He stretched his wrists. He led his mind into the vast empty space from one moment to the next. He studied each discrete instant from when the ball left his pitcher's hand. He moved through the space of his own attentiveness. The ball left the Brazilian's sacred bat, and in two moments the shortstop was on his knees, the ball in his left hand. With his right hand he snapped his fingers to catch the attention of the first baseman, who had no idea where the ball had gone. The first baseman looked, and the shortstop threw the ball to his glove exactly. The stadium dropped to its knees. No one knew what to think. It was as if the shortstop had pulled a ball out of the nothingness, that a ball had disappeared off the end of the Brazilian's holy bat and a new one appeared in the shortstop's hand. He'd broken his pinkie fingertip.

For six innings, the shortstop performed miracles. He caught the ball like a conjurer, each time more abstractedly. As he studied each instant more meticulously, and lingered longer in each one, the ball became secondary. He was watching for patterns of glimmer in his teammates' eyes, noting irregularities in the gentle odor of peanut skins blowing onto the field. The shortstop fell irrevocably in love with the slowness of time.

With one out in the top of the eighth, his team losing eleven to four, the ball hanging in mid-pitch, halfway to the plate, the shortstop grabbed the ball out of the air by a loose thread and left the stadium.

The sacred bat swung at nothing and they looked to the shortstop for the ball. But he was gone forever, and the ball with him.

Fifty-two. Isabella's Omissions

When Penelope woke from her nap, Isabella was gone. Gone, too, was the magnetic tape that had recorded Isabella's speaking. A few technicians were working away in the devices room, oblivious to the disappearance. A fortune cookie sat on the floor where Isabella had been. She opened it and read the slip of paper. *A lucky detective is the one with many pending mysteries.* On the back were lucky numbers. They were like no numbers Penelope had ever seen.

Harry the ex-president was disappointed to learn of the dinosaur's disappearance, particularly on account of its synchroneity with the disappearance of his star shortstop. All he had left were his dreams of Valentina Tereshkova.

Benjamin made Penelope a lunch of crêpes suzettes and raspberries. "Can you explain this disappearance?" he asked her.

"She could speak English," Penelope said. "She talked to me this morning." Penelope told Benjamin everything Isabella had said to her. Benjamin stared at Penelope's eyebrows, with a thirsty look on his face. "Do you not believe me?" asked Penelope.

"I don't care whether I believe you or not. You're good girl and you've always been a good girl. As for the rest of it, I do not give a damn," said Benjamin. He went on staring at her eyebrows, looking desperately thirsty. Once she gave up on him saying anything else, he said, "Do me this one favor and don't talk about that dinosaur ever again."

Isabella had not told Penelope a single untrue thing. She had, however, allowed notable omissions. She did not mention, for example, that among the first generation of dinosaurs, two-thirds died before they turned six months old, and she didn't mention that no one honestly believed the project would work in the first place, and that when all the baby dinosaurs were dying, they took it as proof that the project would fail utterly, and that this was how the old humans had died off, certain of their failure to perpetuate. It didn't seem worth mentioning to Isabella. They were her ancestors' indecorous last thoughts, to keep private.

Isabella also neglected to mention how she herself had ended up frozen in the ice, that Isabella had inherited something of Beth's predictive proclivity, and that Isabella knew what was coming for the dinosaurs, that after a few hundred generations, their genetic material was starting to decompose, that it had done a beautiful job, but it was too big and awkward to stick together like proper genes, that the glue of their programming was coming undone, that they had been a very good and noble idea, but they were finding their moment of impracticability. In a few generations they would lay empty eggs, some of which are still intact today, buried just a few feet in the ground, waiting for someone to come by and crack them and let out their gravid air. Isabella neglected to mention that she was acting on her own doomsday precognition when she swam down to Antarctica and stored herself away, certain of her eventual discovery. Isabella neglected to mention it because now, on the other side of the extinction, safe and wondrous, she had no idea what to do with herself.

Fifty-three. Eliza and Dissent

The statisticians tried to keep Beth more or less a secret. They announced her predictions, but they equivocated about the existence of the girl herself. They referred to her as "our new technology," saying things like, "Our new technology strongly suggests that a traffic helicopter will make an emergency landing on the interstate Wednesday at lunchtime," and so on. It was unlike the statisticians, who generally tended to elucidate their methods to exhaustion. But when Beth predicted the human extinction, the statisticians decided to explain themselves. They brought her to a televised conference and explained her talent and broke her unfortunate news to the television viewership. No one could doubt the statisticians, who had proven themselves infallible.

Eliza's first look at Beth was in a newspaper photo the day after the televised conference. In the picture, Beth had her hair done up in a bun on the top of her head like a balancing act. Eliza wore her hair in the same bun, and the sight of it perched on her little clone's head made her want to cry, though she hadn't cried in many years, and now she strained to, but could not. She'd seen the moment coming, and though the sensation of her premonitions coming into reality still moved and almost even surprised her, and this one more than any other, which she'd held onto in her mind like a talisman for almost Beth's whole life, still she was too ready for it to cry.

Instead, she did what she knew she would do. She talked to a newspaper. She told the newspaper how she had an innate knack for speculating perfectly on future events, just like the little girl who worked for the statisticians. In fact, she told the newspaper, you may notice the similarity in physical appearance between the little girl and myself. That, said Eliza to the newspaper, is because the girl is my exact genetic copy. Some years ago, the statisticians offered me a position making predictions for them. You may remember the stories at the time, about a little girl who'd successfully predicted a handful of very unlikely events. For personal reasons, I stopped announcing my predictions. But they have never stopped occurring to me. They occur to me almost overwhelmingly. And I have kept them quietly to myself.

Now, said Eliza to the newspaper, I feel obliged to share one. I love my clone dearly, though we have never met and never will. I suspect that we may be the only ones capable of properly understanding one another. But this momentous decision she's made, that humans have no chance at surviving, is incorrect. We're on the verge of developing technologies subtle and wonderful enough to save us from the damage our older, primitive technology has made. We can survive. And quite happily. Humans are on the verge of enjoying an unprecedented level of general prosperity.

The newspaper printed everything Eliza told it. Perhaps because everyone wanted so much to believe Eliza, nobody believed her. Almost nobody. About fifty thousand people believed her. The whole bunch of them got together on a little island city down by the Falklands, and they hid from the fairies. One of them was the very same scientist who had invented fairies. He had a terrific little laboratory. When the island started sinking into the Atlantic, he built an enormous bubble around it. When they got tired of their underwater city, he built them a great big rocket and they all got in and took off to look for a new planet.

The new planet was beautiful, and the scientist hero now dedicated himself to improving the human biology. He fixed our biology up so that now no one dies unless they really want to. Then he wiped his hands and gave up science. He decided to make himself a daughter. That was the last thing he wanted. Instead, he ended up with twenty-nine sons, of whom I am the youngest.

Fifty-four. My Telescope

Once my father gave up hope of having a daughter, he died. Of his own will, of course, since no one here dies any other way. I think there was something fulfilling about it for him, finally to want something with no chance of getting it. I was a baby when he died, the last in his long line of misgendered children. No one knows how old he was. The whole planet lost track of time a long time ago.

My mother stayed alive to finish raising me. She doted on me. All my twenty-eight brothers are idiots. They lie around in a pile like human socks. Occasionally one of them starts up groaning, and then they all start groaning. Then, one by one, they fall asleep and go quiet. When she reckoned I was sufficiently grown, my mother followed my father into the afterlife.

I used whatever scientific facility I've inherited from my father to build my telescope. It's something beyond what he would have imagined possible, I think. I can look unobscured at any distance in any direction. Through obstructions. I can look in directions the human senses can't ordinarily even detect, let alone focus on. I can watch anything's thoughts and memories just as I might watch an amateur opera. It's with my telescope that I see into the afterlife to check on Iple, or my mother and father. My father had very little expectation for an afterlife. In fact, he was certain of its nonexistence. He still inhabits it in disbelief.

From watching life on Earth, I have recovered some sense of time, though I still notice it awkwardly, as though I'm writing with the wrong hand. Moreover, I'm afraid that my consciousness of time may be ruining me. I look over at my brothers, unaged, like perfect moron-cherubs. I, on the other hand, am growing creases in my eyes. My stomach mounts the occasional rebellion against the rest of me.

Everything I've reported, I've reported on the authority of my telescope. Any inaccuracies are a product of the telescope's shortcomings. Of which I can detect none. It's proven itself infinitely agile. At least, it's no less agile than my eye.

Fifty-five. Harry & Valentina

Valentina's face is plain and hard. She has lips like chalk. Her eyes are nearly impossible to remember. Harry wakes up and tries to remember from his dream the look of her eyes, or even the color. He can't do it. Her irises are gray. Her pupils, too, are gray, not black. An intermediate, shadowy gray. They slip through the memory like eels.

Harry is a useless man now when he's awake. He eats only sardine sandwiches with ketchup, and watches historical documentaries on the television. He lives for his dreams, which are devoted to Valentina. He begs her to call him Harry, and she flushes and demurs. She cannot possibly call him Harry. He begs her again. He offers her his golden molar as a token of his devotion, which she cannot accept. He removes a bit of grenade, buried deep in his shoulder. Against his better judgment he offers her his eyes, to wear like jewelry. Valentina shudders. He is irrecoverably fictional to her, even in his own dreams, where she herself is part fiction.

She's fleeing him now, coasting into space in her Soviet spacesuit, under which she wears a modest white blouse and a modest olive skirt, her hair in a bun. Harry must have her intimacy, which he estimates is roughly more interminable than space itself. He makes chase, wearing not even a spacesuit, only his pajamas and slippers. He will do everything in his power not to wake up from this dream. His slippers are slowing him down, and he kicks them off to dance with each other, barely gravitated, lost in the mildest weightfulness in the universe.

Harry has brought a great shimmering length of pink ribbon with him, and he strings it up across the cosmos through his pursuit of Valentina, either to decorate space for her or to catch her in it, he doesn't know which. He holds his breath. It's easy. His breath doesn't even want to get out. Valentina is a distant speck among the stars. Maybe she's decided to hide out behind one. Harry will not lose her tracks. He readies his mind for her intelligence, whatever unknowable intelligence, to occupy him.

And he kicks his legs dauntlessly to propel himself onward, as though he were roller-skating. Watching it, I continue to harbor a slight suspicion that someone might yet fall permanently in love.

Fifty-six. Epilogue

First, there's Gottlieb. Gottlieb for whom Zebedee bought a Go set. The Go set had some of Zebedee's luck leaked into it, and Gottlieb became a master. The board seduced him and he in his turn seduced the pieces. He could seduce his opponents' pieces into admitting their deep secret faults. He played only against the great masters, who were helpless against him. Then he played only against himself, in matches too sophisticated for anyone else to recognize their brilliance. Gottlieb neglected his mother and his wife until they disappeared from him forever. Meanwhile he broke his own heart, over and over, with inexpressible elegance, on his Go board.

His wife disguised herself as a man and lived among pirates as a pirate. She remained fair-faced. Even for a woman she had a fair face. But she was agile and merciless. Her reputation was for cutting off earlobes and swallowing them. The gesture was so inexplicable that it inevitably struck terror. Other pirates feared her violently, and this, they thought, explained their strong sexual urges for her. She died by snakebite. Gottlieb's mother, though, died quietly of a stroke behind the counter of her pizzeria.

Then there is Asa. During his trial for murdering Iple, he set his own head on fire.

There is the goldbeater. The goldbeater had perpetually cold hands and feet. They were cold as streamwater. Frauds shivered when they met the goldbeater. He may reappear. We might look for him in any of a million places.

There are disappearances. The shortstop has disappeared, and Isabella. And Harry's son, Louis. What great thing might Louis do? I have a feeling some terrific catastrophe is in store. Some world-stopping turn of events. Perhaps my twenty-eight brothers will wake up and find their purpose. They were never limp idiots after all, they were simply waiting for their moment. They will set sail for your planet. They have awful, miraculous technology, a fluency with those exotic things of the universe about which you can only speculate like a child. In the moment of catastrophe, it will be only those who seem to have disappeared from the Earth who might save it. The critical moment of heroism for the painfully forgotten or misplaced souls.

No, my brothers are lobotomous. They will not set sail for your planet. I will simply go on watching it, wondering after Louis, who seems out of range of even my telescope, perpetually missing.

There is the figurehead, catching dust and light in Zebedee's empty house, filling up with souls, like it's getting ready for something. There is an undeniable getting ready for something. Perhaps Louis will roam and stumble into Zebedee's old house and crack the figurehead open like a piñata, for a great unhousing of souls, an unburdening of that unlocatable, irresistible imbalance. Or he may crack it open to no effect whatsoever.

Penelope has given up her detective persona.

Iple has very little to do. He whistles, kicks his heels once in a while so as not to weep depravedly, of which he has already done considerably more than his share.

Fifty-seven. Second Epilogue

Things have been gradually dropping out of my ken, or the ken of my telescope. There is no sign of the shortstop, or Isabella. This morning, I couldn't find the afterlife where I remembered it. In fact, when I blink into the eyepiece, all I make out is the reflection of my own blinking eye, as though I've left the lens cap on. But I have no lens cap.

My guess was that something jarred the mirrors and lenses out of alignment inside the telescope, but no, I checked, it's all perfect inside. My confidence is unbuckling. Either my eye has lost its focal reflexes entirely, or some hidden switch has been turned, and the gracious circumstance I presumed as the invi-olable way, that the world should be visible to me, no longer applies. The distant world, even the merely semi-distant world, has stopped speaking to me. But I have the thread of a suspi-cion that it never spoke in the first place, that my telescope has always been hopelessly darkened, and that anything I gleaned from it was gleaned out of a nonfunctioning nothingness. I have a guess that it's more a kaleidoscope than a telescope, something with which to examine the dancing that goes on in my own eye. I have an inkling that my father had good reason to disbelieve in the afterlife, and good reason to quit the world when he did.

Thankfully, the telescope is not my only invention. There's a magic blanket I'm ready to test. You cover yourself entirely with the blanket, and when you take the blanket off, you've disappeared. Then, you stuff the blanket into your fist, and when you open your fist, the blanket's gone.

Fifty-eight. Travel in the Mouth of the Wolf

I would like to wax philosophical. There are endless routes to death. There is death by strangulation from the umbilical cord, before even leaving the uterus. There is death by frailty in the newborn, newborns with hearts the size of fingerprints. There is death by playing too long in the autumn rain. There is death by the infection of a wound. There is death by bugbite. There is death by venereal disease. There is death by madness. There is death by trampling. There is death born from the lungs, death born from the heart, and death born from the brain, seemingly out of nothing. There is death by falling down the stairs. There is death by falling down just one stair. There is death by falling with no stairs anywhere in sight. There is death by just sitting down. There is death by ingenuity. There is death by shark attack. There is death by the killer bee. There is death by poisonous smell. There is death by one of the many death machines, such as a guillotine or a bomb or a crowd with stones. There is death by simple mistake. There is death by catching a piece of jewelry in the fast-moving parts of a piece of heavy industrial equipment, such as a necklace in a printing press. And there is dismemberment and disfigurement. You're right to imagine yourself a pitifully frail thing hurled into the perilous cold forest night. You are on a trip from one bit of darkness to another bit of darkness, with danger and darkness in between. Maybe you have a window, or a few windows, to look out. Keep your window clean. An unclean window is like a depression. Stay away from the window during tornados. A tornado wind can blow glass shards just like they were bullets. Find a wolf who won't swallow you, and ask if you might climb into its mouth to make your trip. That way you at least stand a chance.

Paul Fattaruso received his MFA in poetry from the University of Massachusetts in 2003. He lives with his wife Kristin in Denver, Colorado, where he is pursuing a PhD. He rides a silver bicycle. As a minister, he has performed one marriage.